Diana Of The Crossways Book 3

by
George Meredith

Diana Of The Crossways Book 3
by George Meredith

Copyright © 2023

All Rights reserved.
No part of this publication may be reproduced, stored in a retrieval system, or transmitted in any form or by any means, electronic, mechanical, photocopying or Otherwise, without the written permission of the publisher.

The author/editor asserts the moral right to be identified as the author/editor of this work.

ISBN: 978-93-57485-05-0

Published by
DOUBLE 9 BOOKS
2/13-B, Ansari Road
Daryaganj, New Delhi – 110002
info@double9books.com
www.double9books.com
Tel. 011-40042856

This book is under public domain

ABOUT THE AUTHOR

George Meredith OM (February 12, 1828-May 18, 1909) was born in Portsmouth, United Kingdom. He was an English poet, writer, and author, whose books are noted for their intelligence, extraordinary dialogues, and aphoristic way of writing. Meredith's books are also recognised for psychological studies of character and a highly subjective perspective on life that is a long way ahead of its time, considering women are equals to men in all streams. His most popular works are The Ordeal of Richard Feverel (1859) and The Egoist (1879). He was nominated for the Nobel Prize in Literature seven times.

CONTENTS

CHAPTER XVIII.
    THE AUTHORESS 7

CHAPTER XIX.
    A DRIVE IN SUNLIGHT AND
    A DRIVE IN MOONLIGHT 15

CHAPTER XX.
    DIANA A NIGHT-WATCH IN
    THE CHAMBER OF DEATH 24

CHAPTER XXI.
    'THE YOUNG MINISTER OF STATE' 34

CHAPTER XXII.
    BETWEEN DIANA AND DACIER:
    THE WIND EAST OVER BLEAK LAND 45

CHAPTER XXIII.
    RECORDS A VISIT TO DIANA FROM
    ONE OF THE WORLD'S GOOD WOMEN 54

CHAPTER XXIV.
    INDICATES A SOUL PREPARED
    FOR DESPERATION 64

CHAPTER XXV.
ONCE MORE THE CROSSWAYS AND
A CHANGE OF TURNINGS..70

CHAPTER XXVI.
IN WHICH A DISAPPOINTED LOVER RECEIVES A
MULTITUDE OF LESSONS..79

CHAPTER XVIII.
THE AUTHORESS

The effect of a great success upon Diana, at her second literary venture, was shown in the transparent sedateness of a letter she wrote to Emma Dunstane, as much as in her immediate and complacent acceptance of the magical change of her fortunes. She spoke one thing and acted another, but did both with a lofty calm that deceived the admiring friend who clearly saw the authoress behind her mask, and feared lest she should be too confidently trusting to the powers of her pen to support an establishment.

'If the public were a perfect instrument to strike on, I should be tempted to take the wonderful success of my PRINCESS at her first appearance for a proof of natural aptitude in composition, and might think myself the genius. I know it to be as little a Stradivarius as I am a Paganini. It is an eccentric machine, in tune with me for the moment, because I happen to have hit it in the ringing spot. The book is a new face appealing to a mirror of the common surface emotions; and the kitchen rather than the dairy offers an analogy for the real value of that "top-skim." I have not seen what I consider good in the book once mentioned among the laudatory notices—except by your dear hand, my Emmy. Be sure I will stand on guard against the "vaporous generalizations," and other "tricks" you fear. Now that you are studying Latin for an occupation—how good and wise it was of Mr. Redworth to propose it!— I look upon you with awe as a classic authority and critic. I wish I had leisure to study with you. What I do is nothing like so solid and durable.

'THE PRINCESS EGERIA' originally (I must have written word of it to you— I remember the evening off Palermo!) was conceived as a sketch; by gradations she grew into a sort of semi-Scudery romance, and swelled to her present portliness. That was done by a great deal of piecing, not to say puffing, of her frame. She would be healthier and have a chance of living longer if she were reduced by a reversal of the processes. But how would the judicious clippings and prickings affect our "pensive public"? Now that I have furnished a house and have a fixed address, under the paws of creditors, I feel I am in the wizard-circle of my popularity and subscribe to its laws or waken to incubus and the desert. Have I been rash? You do not pronounce. If I have bound myself to pipe as others please, it need not be entirely; and I can promise you it shall not be; but still I am sensible when I lift my "little quill" of having forced the note of a woodland wren into the popular nightingale's—which may end in the daw's, from straining; or worse, a toy-whistle.

'That is, in the field of literature. Otherwise, within me deep, I am not aware of any transmutation of the celestial into coined gold. I sound myself, and ring clear. Incessant writing is my refuge, my solace—escape out of the personal net. I delight in it, as in my early morning walks at Lugano, when I went threading the streets and by the lake away to "the heavenly mount," like a dim idea worming upward in a sleepy head to bright wakefulness.

'My anonymous critic, of whom I told you, is intoxicating with eulogy. The signature "Apollonius" appears to be of literary-middle indication. He marks passages approved by you. I have also had a complimentary letter from Mr. Dacier:

'For an instance of this delight I have in writing, so strong is it that I can read pages I have written, and tear the stuff to strips (I did yesterday), and resume, as if nothing had happened. The waves within are ready for any displacement. That must be a good sign. I do not doubt of excelling my PRINCESS; and if she received compliments, the next may hope for more. Consider, too, the novel pleasure of earning money by the labour we delight in. It is an answer to your question whether I am happy. Yes, as the savage islander before the ship entered the bay with the fire-water. My blood is wine, and I have the slumbers of an infant. I dream, wake, forget my dream, barely dress before the pen is galloping; barely breakfast; no toilette till noon. A savage in good sooth! You see, my Emmy, I could not house with the "companionable person" you hint at. The poles can never come together till the earth is crushed. She would find my habits intolerable, and I hers contemptible, though we might both be companionable persons. My dear, I could not even live with myself.

My blessed little quill, which helps me divinely to live out of myself, is and must continue to be my one companion. It is my mountain height, morning light, wings, cup from the springs, my horse, my goal, my lancet and replenisher, my key of communication with the highest, grandest, holiest between earth and heaven-the vital air connecting them.

'In justice let me add that I have not been troubled by hearing of any of the mysterious legal claims, et caetera. I am sorry to hear bad reports of health. I wish him entire felicity—no step taken to bridge division! The thought of it makes me tigrish.

'A new pianist playing his own pieces (at Lady Singleby's concert) has given me exquisite pleasure' and set me composing songs—not to his music, which could be rendered only by sylphs moving to "soft recorders" in the humour of wildness, languor, bewitching caprices, giving a new sense to melody. How I wish you had been with me to hear him! It was the most AEolian thing ever caught from a night-breeze by the soul of a poet.

'But do not suppose me having headlong tendencies to the melting mood. (The above, by the way, is a Pole settled in Paris, and he is to be introduced to me at Lady Pennon's.)—What do you say to my being invited by Mr. Whitmonby to aid him in writing leading articles for the paper he is going to conduct! "write as you talk and it will do," he says. I am choosing my themes. To write—of politics—as I talk, seems to me like an effort to jump away from my shadow. The black dog of consciousness declines to be shaken off. If some one commanded me to talk as I write! I suspect it would be a way of winding me up to a sharp critical pitch rapidly.

'Not good news of Lord D. I have had messages. Mr. Dacier conceals his alarm. The PRINCESS gave great gratification. She did me her best service there. Is it not cruel that the interdict of the censor should force me to depend for information upon such scraps as I get from a gentleman passing my habitation on his way to the House? And he is not, he never has been, sympathetic in that direction. He sees my grief, and assumes an undertakerly air, with some notion of acting in concert, one supposes little imagining how I revolt from that crape-hatband formalism of sorrow!

'One word of her we call our inner I. I am not drawing upon her resources for my daily needs; not wasting her at all, I trust; certainly not walling her up, to deafen her voice. It would be to fall away from you. She bids me sign myself, my beloved, ever, ever your Tony.'

The letter had every outward show of sincereness in expression, and was endowed to wear that appearance by the writer's impulse to protest with so resolute a vigour as to delude herself. Lady Dunstane heard of Mr. Dacier's novel attendance at concerts. The world made a note of it; for the gentleman was notoriously without ear for music.

Diana's comparison of her hours of incessant writing to her walks under the dawn at Lugano, her boast of the similarity of her delight in both, deluded her uncorrupted conscience to believe that she was now spiritually as free: as in that fair season of the new spring in her veins. She, was not an investigating physician, nor was Lady Dunstane, otherwise they would have examined the material points of her conduct— indicators of the spiritual secret always. What are the patient's acts? The patient's, mind was projected too far beyond them to see the fore finger they stretched at her; and the friend's was not that of a prying doctor on the look out for betraying symptoms. Lady Dunstane did ask herself why Tony should have incurred the burden of a costly household— a very costly: Sir Lukin had been at one of Tony's little' dinners: but her wish to meet the world on equal terms, after a long dependency, accounted for it in seeming to excuse. The guests on the occasion were Lady Pennon. Lady Singleby, Mr. Whitmonby, Mr. Percy Dacier, Mr. Tonans; —'Some other woman,' Sir Lukin said, and himself. He reported the cookery as matching the: conversation, and that was princely; the wines not less—an extraordinary fact to note of a woman. But to hear Whitmonby and Diana Warwick! How he told a story, neat as a postman's knock, and she tipped it with a remark and ran to a second, drawing in Lady Pennon, and then Dacier, 'and me!' cried Sir Lukin; 'she made us all toss the ball from hand to hand, and all talk up to the mark; and none of us noticed that we all went together to the drawing-room, where we talked for another hour, and broke up fresher than we began.'

'That break between the men and the women after dinner was Tony's aversion, and I am glad she has instituted a change,' said Lady Dunstane.

She heard also from Redworth of the unexampled concert of the guests at Mrs. Warwick's dinner parties. He had met on one occasion the Esquarts, the Pettigrews, Mr. Percy Dacier, and a Miss Paynham.

Redworth had not a word to say of the expensive household. Whatever Mrs. Warwick did was evidently good to him. On another evening the party was composed of Lady Pennon, Lord Larrian, Miss Paynham, a clever Mrs. Wollasley, Mr. Henry Wilmers, and again Mr. Percy Dacier.

When Diana came to Copsley, Lady Dunstane remarked on the recurrence of the name of Miss Paynham in the list of her guests.

'And Mr. Percy Dacier's too,' said Diana, smiling. 'They are invited each for specific reasons. It pleases Lord Dannisburgh to hear that a way has been found to enliven his nephew; and my little dinners are effective, I think. He wakes. Yesterday evening he capped flying jests with Mr. Sullivan Smith. But you speak of Miss. Paynham.' Diana lowered her voice on half a dozen syllables, till the half-tones dropped into her steady look. 'You approve, Emmy?'

The answer was: 'I do—true or not.'

'Between us two, dear, I fear! . . . In either case, she has been badly used. Society is big engine enough to protect itself. I incline with British juries to do rough justice to the victims. She has neither father nor brother. I have had no confidences: but it wears the look of a cowardly business. With two words in his ear, I could arm an Irishman to do some work of chastisement: he would select the rascal's necktie for a cause of quarrel and lords have to stand their ground as well as commoners. They measure the same number of feet when stretched their length. However, vengeance with the heavens! though they seem tardy. Lady Pennon has been very kind about it; and the Esquarts invite her to Lockton. Shoulder to shoulder, the tide may be stemmed.'

'She would have gone under, but for you, dear Tony!' said Emma' folding arms round her darling's neck anal kissing her. 'Bring her here some day.'

Diana did not promise it. She had her vision of Sir Lukin in his fit of lunacy.

'I am too weak for London now,' Emma resumed. 'I should like to be useful. Is she pleasant?'

'Sprightly by nature. She has worn herself with fretting.'

'Then bring her to stay with me, if I cannot keep you. She will talk of you to me.'

'I will bring her for a couple of days,' Diana said. 'I am too busy to remain longer. She paints portraits to amuse herself. She ought to be pushed, wherever she is received about London, while the season is warm. One season will suffice to establish her. She is pretty, near upon six and twenty: foolish, of course:—she pays for having had a romantic head. Heavy payment, Emmy! I drive at laws, but hers is an instance of the creatures wanting simple human kindness.'

'The good law will come with a better civilization; but before society can be civilized it has to be debarbarized,' Emma remarked, and Diana sighed over the task and the truism.

I should have said in younger days, because it will not look plainly on our nature and try to reconcile it with our conditions. But now I see that the sin is cowardice. The more I know of the world the more clearly I perceive that its top and bottom sin is cowardice, physically and morally alike. Lord Larrian owns to there being few heroes in an army. We must fawn in society. What is the meaning of that dread of one example of tolerance? O my dear! let us give it the right name. Society is the best thing we have, but it is a crazy vessel worked by a crew that formerly practised piracy, and now, in expiation, professes piety, fearful of a discovered Omnipotence, which is in the image of themselves and captain. Their old habits are not quite abandoned, and their new one is used as a lash to whip the exposed of us for a propitiation of the capricious potentate whom they worship in the place of the true God.'

Lady Dunstane sniffed. 'I smell the leading article.'

Diana joined with her smile, 'No, the style is rather different.'

'Have you not got into a trick of composing in speaking, at times?'

Diana confessed, 'I think I have at times. Perhaps the daily writing of all kinds and the nightly talking . . . I may be getting strained.'

'No, Tony; but longer visits in the country to me would refresh you. I miss your lighter touches. London is a school, but, you know it, not a school for comedy nor for philosophy; that is gathered on my hills, with London distantly in view, and then occasional descents on it well digested.'

'I wonder whether it is affecting me!' said Diana, musing. 'A metropolitan hack! and while thinking myself free, thrice harnessed; and all my fun gone. Am I really as dull as a tract, my dear? I must be, or I should be proving the contrary instead of asking. My pitfall is to fancy I have powers equal to the first look-out of the eyes of the. morning. Enough of me. We talked of Mary Paynham. If only some right good man would marry her!'

Lady Dunstane guessed at the right good man in Diana's mind. 'Do you bring them together?'

Diana nodded, and then shook doleful negatives to signify no hope.

'None whatever—if we mean the same person,' said Lady Dunstane, bethinking her, in the spirit of wrath she felt at such a scheme being planned by Diana to snare the right good man, that instead of her own true lover Redworth, it might be only Percy Dacier. So filmy of mere sensations are these little ideas as they flit in converse, that she did not reflect on her friend's ignorance of Redworth's love of her, or on the unlikely choice of one in Dacier's high station to reinstate a damsel.

They did not name the person.

'Passing the instance, which is cruel, I will be just to society thus far,' said Diana. 'I was in a boat at Richmond last week, and Leander was revelling along the mud-banks, and took it into his head to swim out to me, and I was moved to take him on board. The ladies in the boat objected, for he was not only wet but very muddy. I was forced to own that their objections were reasonable. My sentimental humaneness had no argument against muslin dresses, though my dear dog's eyes appealed pathetically, and he would keep swimming after us. The analogy excuses the world for protecting itself in extreme cases; nothing, nothing excuses its insensibility to cases which may be pleaded. You see the pirate crew turned pious-ferocious in sanctity.' She added, half laughing: 'I am reminded by the boat, I have unveiled my anonymous critic, and had a woeful disappointment. He wrote like a veteran; he is not much more than a boy. I received a volume of verse, and a few lines begging my acceptance. I fancied I knew the writing, and wrote asking him whether I had not to thank him, and inviting him to call. He seems a nice lad of about two and twenty, mad for literature; and he must have talent. Arthur Rhodes by name. I may have a chance of helping him. He was an articled clerk of Mr. Braddock's, the same who valiantly came to my rescue once. He was with us in the boat.'

'Bring him to me some day,' said Lady Dunstane.

Miss Paynham's visit to Copsley was arranged, and it turned out a failure. The poor young lady came in a flutter, thinking that the friend of Mrs. Warwick would expect her to discourse cleverly. She attempted it, to Diana's amazement. Lady Dunstane's opposingly corresponding stillness provoked Miss Paynham to expatiate, for she had sprightliness and some mental reserves of the common order. Clearly, Lady Dunstane mused while listening amiably, Tony never could have designed this gabbler for the mate of Thomas Redworth!

Percy Dacier seemed to her the more likely one, in that light, and she thought so still, after Sir Lukin had introduced him at Copsley for a couple of days of the hunting season. Tony's manner with him suggested it; she had a dash of leadership. They were not intimate in look or tongue.

But Percy Dacier also was too good for Miss Paynham, if that was Tony's plan for him, Lady Dunstane thought, with the relentlessness of an invalid and recluse's distaste. An aspect of penitence she had not demanded, but the silly gabbier under a stigma she could not pardon.

Her opinion of Miss Paynham was diffused in her silence.

Speaking of Mr. Dacier, she remarked, 'As you say of him, Tony, he can brighten, and when you give him a chance he is entertaining. He has fine gifts. If I were a member of his family I should beat about for a match for him. He strikes me as one of the young men who would do better married.'

'He is doing very well, but the wonder is that he doesn't marry,' said Diana. 'He ought to be engaged. Lady Esquart told me that he was. A Miss Asper—great heiress; and the Daciers want money. However, there it is.'

Not many weeks later Diana could not have spoken of Mr. Percy Dacier with this air of indifference without corruption of her inward guide.

CHAPTER XIX.
A DRIVE IN SUNLIGHT AND A DRIVE IN MOONLIGHT

The fatal time to come for her was in the Summer of that year.

Emma had written her a letter of unwonted bright spirits, contrasting strangely with an inexplicable oppression of her own that led her to imagine her recent placid life the pause before thunder, and to sharp the mood of her solitary friend she flew to Copsley, finding Sir Lukin absent, as usual. They drove out immediately after breakfast, on one of those high mornings of the bared bosom of June when distances are given to our eyes, and a soft air fondles leaf and grass-blade, and beauty and peace are overhead, reflected, if we will. Rain had fallen in the night. Here and there hung a milk-white cloud with folded sail. The South-west left it in its bay of blue, and breathed below. At moments the fresh scent of herb and mould swung richly in warmth. The young beech-leaves glittered, pools of rain-water made the roadways laugh, the grass-banks under hedges rolled their interwoven weeds in cascades of many-shaded green to right and left of the pair of dappled ponies, and a squirrel crossed ahead, a lark went up a little way to ease his heart, closing his wings when the burst was over, startled black-birds, darting with a clamour like a broken cockcrow, looped the wayside woods from hazel to oak-scrub; short flights, quick spirts everywhere, steady sunshine above.

Diana held the reins. The whip was an ornament, as the plume of feathers to the general officer. Lady Dunstane's ponies were a present from Redworth, who always chose the pick of the land for his gifts. They joyed in their trot, and were the very love-birds of the breed for their pleasure of going together, so like that Diana called them the Dromios. Through an old gravel-cutting a gateway led to the turf of the down, springy turf bordered on a long line, clear as a racecourse, by golden gorse covers, and leftward over the gorse the dark ridge of the fir and heath country ran companionably to the Southwest, the valley between, with undulations of wood and meadow sunned or shaded, clumps, mounds, promontories, away to broad spaces of tillage banked by wooded hills, and dimmer beyond and farther, the faintest shadowiness of heights, as a veil to the illimitable. Yews, junipers, radiant beeches, and gleams of the service-tree or the white-beam spotted the semicircle of swelling green Down black and silver. The sun in the valley sharpened his beams on squares of buttercups, and made a pond a diamond.

'You see, Tony,' Emma said, for a comment on the scene, 'I could envy Italy for having you, more than you for being in Italy.'

'Feature and colour!' said Diana. 'You have them here, and on a scale that one can embrace. I should like to build a hut on this point, and wait for such a day to return. It brings me to life.' She lifted her eyelids on her friend's worn sweet face, and knowing her this friend up to death, past it in her hopes, she said bravely, 'It is the Emma of days and scenes to me! It helps me to forget myself, as I do when I think of you, dearest; but the subject has latterly been haunting me, I don't know why, and ominously, as if my nature were about to horrify my soul. But I am not sentimentalizing, you are really this day and scene in my heart.'

Emma smiled confidingly. She spoke her reflection: 'The heart must be troubled a little to have the thought. The flower I gather here tells me that we may be happy in privation and suffering if simply we can accept beauty. I won't say expel the passions, but keep passion sober, a trotter in harness.'

Diana caressed the ponies' heads with the droop of her whip: 'I don't think I know him!' she said.

Between sincerity and a suspicion so cloaked and dull that she did not feel it to be the opposite of candour, she fancied she was passionless because she could accept the visible beauty, which was Emma's prescription and test; and she forced herself to make much of it, cling to it, devour it; with envy of Emma's contemplative happiness, through whose grave mind she tried to get to the peace in it, imagining that she succeeded. The cloaked and dull suspicion weighed within her nevertheless. She took it for a mania to speculate on herself. There are states of the crimson blood when the keenest wits are childish, notably in great-hearted women aiming at the majesty of their sex and fearful of confounding it by the look direct and the downright word. Yet her nature compelled her inwardly to phrase the sentence: 'Emma is a wife!' The character of her husband was not considered, nor was the meaning of the exclamation pursued.

They drove through the gorse into wild land of heath and flowering hawthorn, and along by tracts of yew and juniper to another point, jutting on a furzy sand-mound, rich with the mild splendour of English scenery, which Emma stamped on her friend's mind by saying: 'A cripple has little to envy in you who can fly when she has feasts like these at her doors.'

They had an inclination to boast on the drive home of the solitude they had enjoyed; and just then, as the road in the wood wound under great beeches, they beheld a London hat. The hat was plucked from its head. A clear-faced youth, rather flushed, dusty at the legs, addressed Diana.

'Mr. Rhodes!' she said, not discouragingly.

She was petitioned to excuse him; he thought she would wish to hear the news in town last night as early as possible; he hesitated and murmured it.

Diana turned to Emma: 'Lord Dannisburgh!' her paleness told the rest.

Hearing from Mr. Rhodes that he had walked the distance from town, and had been to Copsley, Lady Dunstane invited him to follow the pony-carriage thither, where he was fed and refreshed by a tea-breakfast, as he preferred walking on tea, he said. 'I took the liberty to call at Mrs. Warwick's house,' he informed her, 'the footman said she was at Copsley. I found it on the map—I knew the directions—and started about two in the morning. I wanted a walk.'

It was evident to her that he was one of the young squires bewitched whom beautiful women are constantly enlisting. There was no concealment of it, though he stirred a sad enviousness in the invalid lady by descanting on the raptures of a walk out of London in the youngest light of day, and on the common objects he had noticed along the roadside, and through the woods, more sustaining, closer with nature than her compulsory feeding on the cream of things.

'You are not fatigued?' she inquired, hoping for that confession at least; but she pardoned his boyish vaunting to walk the distance back without any fatigue at all.

He had a sweeter reward for his pains; and if the business of the chronicler allowed him to become attached to pure throbbing felicity wherever it is encountered, he might be diverted by the blissful unexpectedness of good fortune befalling Mr. Arthur Rhodes in having the honour to conduct Mrs. Warwick to town. No imagined happiness, even in the heart of a young man of two and twenty, could have matched it. He was by her side, hearing and seeing her, not less than four hours. To add to his happiness, Lady Dunstane said she would be glad to welcome him again. She thought him a pleasant specimen of the self-vowed squire.

Diana was sure that there would be a communication for her of some sort at her house in London; perhaps a message of farewell from the dying lord, now dead. Mr. Rhodes had only the news of the evening journals, to the effect that Lord Dannisburgh had expired at his residence, the Priory, Hallowmere, in Hampshire. A message of farewell from him, she hoped for: knowing him as she did, it seemed a certainty; and she hungered for that last gleam of life in her friend. She had no anticipation of the burden of the message awaiting her.

A consultation as to the despatching of the message, had taken place among the members of Lord Dannisburgh's family present at his death. Percy Dacier was one of them, and he settled the disputed point, after some time had been spent in persuading his father to take the plain view of obligation in the matter, and in opposing the dowager countess, his grandmother, by stating that he had already sent a special messenger to London. Lord Dannisburgh on his death-bed had expressed a wish that Mrs. Warwick would sit with him for an hour one night before the nails were knocked in his coffin. He spoke of it twice, putting it the second time to Percy as a formal request to be made to her, and Percy had promised him that Mrs. Warwick should have the message. He had done his best to keep his pledge, aware of the disrelish of the whole family for the lady's name, to say nothing of her presence.

'She won't come,' said the earl.

'She'll come,' said old Lady Dacier.

'If the woman respects herself she'll hold off it,' the earl insisted because of his desire that way. He signified in mutterings that the thing was improper and absurd, a piece of sentiment, sickly senility, unlike Lord Dannisburgh. Also that Percy had been guilty of excessive folly.

To which Lady Dacier nodded her assent, remarking, 'The woman is on her mettle. From what I've heard of her, she's not a woman to stick at trifles. She'll take it as a sort of ordeal by touch, and she 'll come.'

They joined in abusing Percy, who had driven away to another part of the country. Lord Creedmore, the heir of the house, was absent, hunting in America, or he might temporarily have been taken into favour by contrast. Ultimately they agreed that the woman must be allowed to enter the house, but could not be received. The earl was a widower; his mother managed the family, and being hard to convince, she customarily carried her point, save when it involved Percy's freedom of action. She was one of the veterans of her sex that age to toughness; and the 'hysterical fuss' she apprehended in the visit of this woman to Lord Dannisburgh's death- bed and body, did not alarm her. For the sake of the household she determined to remain, shut up in her room. Before night the house was empty of any members of the family excepting old Lady Dacier and the outstretched figure on the bed.

Dacier fled to escape the hearing of the numberless ejaculations re- awakened in the family by his uncle's extraordinary dying request. They were an outrage to the lady, of whom he could now speak as a privileged champion; and the request itself had an air of proving her stainless, a white soul and efficacious advocate at the celestial gates (reading the mind of the dying man). So he thought at one moment: he had thought so when charged with the message to her; had even thought it a natural wish that she should look once on the face she would see no more, and say farewell to it, considering that in life it could not be requested. But the susceptibility to sentimental emotion beside a death-bed, with a dying man's voice in the ear, requires fortification if it is to be maintained;' and the review of his uncle's character did not tend to make this very singular request a proof that the lady's innocence was honoured in it. His epicurean uncle had no profound esteem for the kind of innocence. He had always talked of

Mrs. Warwick—with warm respect for her: Dacier knew that he had bequeathed her a sum of money. The inferences were either way. Lord Dannisburgh never spoke evilly of any woman, and he was perhaps bound to indemnify her materially as well as he could for what she had suffered.—On the other hand, how easy it was to be the dupe of a woman so handsome and clever.—Unlikely too that his uncle would consent to sit at the Platonic banquet with her.—Judging by himself, Dacier deemed it possible for man. He was not quick to kindle, and had lately seen much of her, had found her a Lady Egeria, helpful in counsel, prompting, inspiriting, reviving as well-waters, and as temperately cool: not one sign of native slipperiness. Nor did she stir the mud in him upon which proud man is built. The shadow of the scandal had checked a few shifty sensations rising now and then of their own accord, and had laid them, with the lady's benign connivance. This was good proof in her favour, seeing that she must have perceived of late the besetting thirst he had for her company; and alone or in the medley equally. To see her, hear, exchange ideas with her; and to talk of new books, try to listen to music at the opera and at concerts, and admire her playing of hostess, were novel pleasures, giving him fresh notions of life, and strengthening rather than disturbing the course of his life's business.

At any rate, she was capable of friendship. Why not resolutely believe that she had been his uncle's true and simple friend! He adopted the resolution, thanking her for one recognized fact:—he hated marriage, and would by this time have been in the yoke, but for the agreeable deviation of his path to her society. Since his visit to Copsley, moreover, Lady Dunstane's idolizing, of her friend had influenced him. Reflecting on it, he recovered from the shock which his uncle's request had caused.

Certain positive calculations were running side by side with the speculations in vapour. His messenger would reach her house at about four of the afternoon. If then at home, would she decide to start immediately?—Would she come? That was a question he did not delay to answer. Would she defer the visit? Death replied to that. She would not delay it.

She would be sure to come at once. And what of the welcome she would meet? Leaving the station at London at six in the evening, she might arrive at the Priory, all impediments counted, between ten and eleven at night. Thence, coldly greeted, or not greeted, to the chamber of death.

A pitiable and cruel reception for a woman upon such a mission!

His mingled calculations and meditations reached that exclamatory terminus in feeling, and settled on the picture of Diana, about as clear as light to blinking eyes, but enough for him to realize her being there and alone, woefully alone. The supposition of an absolute loneliness was most possible. He had intended to drive back the next day, when the domestic storm would be over, and take the chances of her coming. It seemed now a piece of duty to return at night, a traverse of twenty rough up and down miles from Itchenford to the heath-land rolling on the chalk wave of the Surrey borders, easily done after the remonstrances of his host were stopped.

Dacier sat in an open carriage, facing a slip of bright moon. Poetical impressions, emotions, any stirrings of his mind by the sensational stamp on it, were new to him, and while he swam in them, both lulled and pricked by his novel accessibility to nature's lyrical touch, he asked himself whether, if he were near the throes of death, the thought of having Diana Warwick to sit beside his vacant semblance for an hour at night would be comforting. And why had his uncle specified an hour of the night? It was a sentiment, like the request: curious in a man so little sentimental. Yonder crescent running the shadowy round of the hoop roused comparisons. Would one really wish to have her beside one in death? In life—ah! But suppose her denied to us in life. Then the desire for her companionship appears passingly comprehensible. Enter into the sentiment, you see that the hour of darkness is naturally chosen. And would even a grand old Pagan crave the presence beside his dead body for an hour of the night of a woman he did not esteem? Dacier answered no. The negative was not echoed in his mind. He repeated it, and to the same deadness.

He became aware that he had spoken for himself, and he had a fit of sourness. For who can say he is not a fool before he has been tried by a woman! Dacier's wretched tendency under vexation to conceive grotesque analogies, anti-poetic, not to say cockney similes, which had slightly chilled Diana at Rovio, set him looking at yonder crescent with the hoop, as at the shape of a white cat climbing a wheel. Men of the northern blood will sometimes lend their assent to poetical images, even to those that do not stun the mind lie bludgeons and imperatively, by much repetition, command their assent; and it is for a solid exchange and interest in usury with soft poetical creatures when they are so condescending; but they are seized by the grotesque. In spite of efforts to efface or supplant it, he saw the white cat, nothing else, even to thinking that she had jumped cleverly to catch the wheel. He was a true descendant of practical hard-grained fighting Northerners, of gnarled dwarf imaginations, chivalrous though they were, and heroes to have serviceable and valiant gentlemen for issue. Without at all tracing back to its origin his detestable image of the white cat on the dead circle, he kicked at the links between his uncle and Diana Warwick, whatever they had been; particularly at the present revival of them. Old Lady Dacier's blunt speech, and his father's fixed opinion, hissed in his head.

They were ignorant of his autumnal visit to the Italian Lakes, after the winter's Nile-boat expedition; and also of the degree of his recent intimacy with Mrs. Warwick; or else, as he knew, he would have heard more hissing things. Her patronage of Miss Paynham exposed her to attacks where she was deemed vulnerable; Lady Dacier muttered old saws as to the flocking of birds; he did not accurately understand it, thought it indiscreet, at best. But in regard to his experience, he could tell himself that a woman more guileless of luring never drew breath. On the contrary, candour said it had always been he who had schemed and pressed for the meeting. He was at liberty to do it, not being bound in honour elsewhere. Besides, despite his acknowledgement of her beauty, Mrs. Warwick was not quite his ideal of the perfectly beautiful woman.

Constance Asper came nearer to it. He had the English taste for red and white, and for cold outlines: he secretly admired a statuesque demeanour with a statue's eyes. The national approbation of a reserved haughtiness in woman, a tempered disdain in her slightly lifted small upperlip and drooped eyelids, was shared by him; and Constance Asper, if not exactly aristocratic by birth, stood well for that aristocratic insular type, which seems to promise the husband of it a casket of all the trusty virtues, as well as the security of frigidity in the casket. Such was Dacier's native taste; consequently the attractions of Diana Warwick for him were, he thought, chiefly mental, those of a Lady Egeria. She might or might not be good, in the vulgar sense. She was an agreeable woman, an amusing companion, very suggestive, inciting, animating; and her past history must be left as her own. Did it matter to him? What he saw was bright, a silver crescent on the side of the shadowy ring. Were it a question of marrying her!—That was out of the possibilities. He remembered, moreover, having heard from a man, who professed to know, that Mrs. Warwick had started in married life by treating her husband cavalierly to an intolerable degree: 'Such as no Englishman could stand,' the portly old informant thundered, describing it and her in racy vernacular. She might be a devil of a wife. She was a pleasant friend; just the soft bit sweeter than male friends which gave the flavour of sex without the artful seductions. He required them strong to move him.

He looked at last on the green walls of the Priory, scarcely supposing a fair watcher to be within; for the contrasting pale colours of dawn had ceased to quicken the brilliancy of the crescent, and summer daylight drowned it to fainter than a silver coin in water. It lay dispieced like a pulled rag. Eastward, over Surrey, stood the full rose of morning. The Priory clock struck four. When the summons of the bell had gained him admittance, and he heard that Mrs. Warwick had come in the night, he looked back through the doorway at the rosy colour, and congratulated himself to think that her hour of watching was at an end. A sleepy footman was his informant. Women were in my lord's dressing-room, he said. Upstairs, at the death-chamber, Dacier paused. No sound came to him. He hurried to his own room, paced about, and returned. Expecting to see no one but the dead, he turned the handle, and the two circles of a shaded lamp, on ceiling and on table, met his gaze.

CHAPTER XX.
DIANA A NIGHT-WATCH IN THE CHAMBER OF DEATH

He stepped into the room, and thrilled to hear the quiet voice beside the bed: 'Who is it?'

Apologies and excuses were on his tongue. The vibration of those grave tones checked them.

'It is you,' she said.

She sat in shadow, her hands joined on her lap. An unopened book was under the lamp.

He spoke in an underbreath: 'I have just come. I was not sure I should find you here. Pardon.'

'There is a chair.'

He murmured thanks and entered into the stillness, observing her.

'You have been watching . . . . You must be tired.'

'No.'

'An hour was asked, only one.'

'I could not leave him.'

'Watchers are at hand to relieve you'

'It is better for him to have me.'

The chord of her voice told him of the gulf she had sunk in during the night. The thought of her endurance became a burden.

He let fall his breath for patience, and tapped the floor with his foot.

He feared to discompose her by speaking. The silence grew more fearful, as the very speech of Death between them.

'You came. I thought it right to let you know instantly. I hoped you would come to-morrow'

'I could not delay.'

'You have been sitting alone here since eleven!'

'I have not found it long.'

'You must want some refreshment . . . tea?'

'I need nothing.'

'It can be made ready in a few minutes.'

'I could not eat or drink.'

He tried to brush away the impression of the tomb in the heavily-curtained chamber by thinking of the summer-morn outside; he spoke of it, the rosy sky, the dewy grass, the piping birds. She listened, as one hearing of a quitted sphere.

Their breathing in common was just heard if either drew a deeper breath. At moments his eyes wandered and shut. Alternately in his mind Death had vaster meanings and doubtfuller; Life cowered under the shadow or outshone it. He glanced from her to the figure in the bed, and she seemed swallowed.

He said: 'It is time for you to have rest. You know your room. I will stay till the servants are up.'

She replied: 'No, let this night with him be mine.'

'I am not intruding . . .?'

'If you wish to remain . . .'

No traces of weeping were on her face. The lampshade revealed it colourless, and lustreless her eyes. She was robed in black. She held her hands clasped.

'You have not suffered?'

'Oh, no.'

She said it without sighing: nor was her speech mournful, only brief.

'You have seen death before?'

'I sat by my father four nights. I was a girl then. I cried till I had no more tears.'

He felt a burning pressure behind his eyeballs.

'Death is natural,' he said.

'It is natural to the aged. When they die honoured . . .'

She looked where the dead man lay. 'To sit beside the young, cut off from their dear opening life . . . !' A little shudder swept over her. 'Oh! that!'

'You were very good to come. We must all thank you for fulfilling his wish.'

'He knew it would be my wish.'

Her hands pressed together.

'He lies peacefully!'

'I have raised the lamp on him, and wondered each time. So changeless he lies. But so like a sleep that will wake. We never see peace but in the features of the dead. Will you look? They are beautiful. They have a heavenly sweetness.'

The desire to look was evidently recurrent with her. Dacier rose.

Their eyes fell together on the dead man, as thoughtfully as Death allows to the creatures of sensation.

'And after?' he said in low tones.

'I trust to my Maker,' she replied. 'Do you see a change since he breathed his last?'

'Not any.'

'You were with him?'

'Not in the room. Two minutes later.'

'Who . . .?'

'My father. His niece, Lady Cathairn.'

'If our lives are lengthened we outlive most of those we would have to close our eyes. He had a dear sister.'

'She died some years back.'

'I helped to comfort him for that loss.'

'He told me you did.'

The lamp was replaced on the table.

'For a moment, when I withdraw the light from him, I feel sadness. As if the light we lend to anything were of value to him now!'

She bowed her head deeply. Dacier left her meditation undisturbed. The birds on the walls outside were audible, tweeting, chirping.

He went to the window-curtains and tried the shutter-bars. It seemed to him that daylight would be cheerfuller for her. He had a thirst to behold her standing bathed in daylight.

'Shall I open them?' he asked her.

'I would rather the lamp,' she said.

They sat silently until she drew her watch from her girdle. 'My train starts at half-past six. It is a walk of thirty-five minutes to the station. I did it last night in that time.'

'You walked here in the dark alone?'

'There was no fly to be had. The station-master sent one of his porters with me. We had a talk on the road. I like those men.'

Dacier read the hour by the mantelpiece clock. 'If you must really go by the early train, I will drive you.'

'No, I will walk; I prefer it.'

'I will order your breakfast at once.'

He turned on his heel. She stopped him. 'No, I have no taste for eating or drinking.'

'Pray . . .' said he, in visible distress.

She shook her head. 'I could not. I have twenty minutes longer. I can find my way to the station; it is almost a straight road out of the park- gates.'

His heart swelled with anger at the household for they treatment she had been subjected to, judging by her resolve not to break bread in the house.

They resumed their silent sitting. The intervals for a word to pass between them were long, and the ticking of the time-piece fronting the death-bed ruled the chamber, scarcely varied.

The lamp was raised for the final look, the leave-taking.

Dacier buried his face, thinking many things—the common multitude in insurrection.

'A servant should be told to come now,' she said. 'I have only to put on my bonnet and I am ready.'

'You will take no . . . ?'

'Nothing.'

'It is not too late for a carriage to be ordered.'

'No—the walk!'

They separated.

He roused the two women in the dressing-room, asleep with heads against the wall. Thence he sped to his own room for hat and overcoat, and a sprinkle of cold water. Descending the stairs, he beheld his companion issuing from the chamber of death. Her lips were shut, her eyelids nervously tremulous.

They were soon in the warm sweet open air, and they walked without an interchange of a syllable through the park into the white hawthorn lane, glad to breathe. Her nostrils took long draughts of air, but of the change of, scene she appeared scarcely sensible.

At the park-gates, she said: 'There is no necessity four your coming.'

His answer was: 'I think of myself. I gain something every step I walk with you.'

'To-day is Thursday,' said she. 'The funeral is . . . ?'

'Monday has been fixed. According to his directions, he will lie in the churchyard of his village—not in the family vault.'

'I know,' she said hastily. 'They are privileged who follow him and see the coffin lowered. He spoke of this quiet little resting-place.'

'Yes, it's a good end. I do not wonder at his wish for the honour you have done him. I could wish it too. But more living than dead— that is a natural wish.'

'It is not to be called an honour.'

'I should feel it so-an honour to me.'

'It is a friend's duty. The word is too harsh; it was his friend's desire. He did not ask it so much as he sanctioned it. For to him what has my sitting beside him been!'

'He had the prospective happiness.'

'He knew well that my soul would be with him—as it was last night. But he knew it would be my poor human happiness to see him with my eyes, touch him with my hand, before he passed from our sight.'

Dacier exclaimed: 'How you can love!'

'Is the village church to be seen?' she asked.

'To the right of those elms; that is the spire. The black spot below is a yew. You love with the whole heart when you love.'

'I love my friends,' she replied.

'You tempt me to envy those who are numbered among them.'

'They are not many.'

'They should be grateful.!

'You have some acquaintance with them all.'

'And an enemy? Had you ever one? Do you know of one?'

'Direct and personal designedly? I think not. We give that title to those who are disinclined to us and add a dash of darker colour to our errors. Foxes have enemies in the dogs; heroines of melodramas have their persecuting villains. I suppose that conditions of life exist where one meets the original complexities. The bad are in every rank. The inveterately malignant I have not found. Circumstances may combine to make a whisper as deadly as a blow, though not of such evil design. Perhaps if we lived at a Court of a magnificent despot we should learn that we are less highly civilized than we imagine ourselves; but that is a fire to the passions, and the extreme is not the perfect test. Our civilization counts positive gains—unless you take the melodrama for the truer picture of us. It is always the most popular with the English.— And look, what a month June is! Yesterday morning I was with Lady Dunstane on her heights, and I feel double the age. He was fond of this wild country. We think it a desert, a blank, whither he has gone, because we will strain to see in the utter dark, and nothing can come of that but the bursting of the eyeballs.'

Dacier assented: 'There's no use in peering beyond the limits.'

'No,' said she; 'the effect is like the explaining of things to a dull head—the finishing stroke to the understanding! Better continue to brood. We get to some unravelment if we are left to our own efforts. I quarrel with no priest of any denomination. That they should quarrel among themselves is comprehensible in their wisdom, for each has the specific. But they show us their way of solving the great problem, and we ought to thank them, though one or the other abominate us. You are advised to talk with Lady Dunstane on these themes.

She is perpetually in the antechamber of death, and her soul is perennially sunshine.—See the pretty cottage under the laburnum curls! Who lives there?'

'His gamekeeper, Simon Rofe.'

'And what a playground for the children, that bit of common by their garden-palings! and the pond, and the blue hills over the furzes. I hope those people will not be turned out.'

Dacier could not tell. He promised to do his best for them.

'But,' said she, 'you are the lord here now.'

'Not likely to be the tenant. Incomes are wanted to support even small estates.'

'The reason is good for courting the income.'

He disliked the remark; and when she said presently:

'Those windmills make the landscape homely,' he rejoined: 'They remind one of our wheeling London gamins round the cab from the station.'

'They remind you,' said she, and smiled at the chance discordant trick he had, remembering occasions when it had crossed her.

'This is homelier than Rovio,' she said; 'quite as nice in its way.'

'You do not gather flowers here.'

'Because my friend has these at her feet.'

'May one petition without a rival, then, for a souvenir?'

'Certainly, if you care to have a common buttercup.'

They reached the station, five minutes in advance of the train. His coming manoeuvre was early detected, and she drew from her pocket the little book he had seen lying unopened on the table, and said: 'I shall have two good hours for reading.'

'You will not object? . . . I must accompany you to town. Permit it, I beg. You shall not be worried to talk.'

'No; I came alone and return alone.'

'Fasting and unprotected! Are you determined to take away the worst impression of us? Do not refuse me this favour.'

'As to fasting, I could not eat: and unprotected no woman is in England, if she is a third-class traveller. That is my experience of the class; and I shall return among my natural protectors—the most unselfishly chivalrous to women in the whole world.'

He had set his heart on going with her, and he attempted eloquence in pleading, but that exposed him to her humour; he was tripped.

'It is not denied that you belong to the knightly class,' she said; 'and it is not necessary that you should wear armour and plumes to proclaim it; and your appearance would be ample protection from the drunken sailors travelling, you say, on this line; and I may be deplorably mistaken in imagining that I could tame them. But your knightliness is due elsewhere; and I commit myself to the fortune of war. It is a battle for women everywhere; under the most favourable conditions among my dear common English. I have not my maid with me, or else I should not dare.'

She paid for a third-class ticket, amused by Dacier's look of entreaty and trouble.

'Of course I obey,' he murmured.

'I have the habit of exacting it in matters concerning my independence,' she said; and it arrested some rumbling notions in his head as to a piece of audacity on the starting of the train. They walked up and down the platform till the bell rang and the train came rounding beneath an arch.

'Oh, by the way, may I ask?' he said: 'was it your article in Whitmonby's journal on a speech of mine last week?'

'The guilty writer is confessed.'

'Let me thank you.'

'Don't. But try to believe it written on public grounds—if the task is not too great.'

'I may call?'

'You will be welcome.'

'To tell you of the funeral—the last of him.'

'Do not fail to come.'

She could have laughed to see him jumping on the steps of the third-class carriages one after another to choose her company for her. In those pre- democratic blissful days before the miry Deluge, the opinion of the requirements of poor English travellers entertained by the Seigneur Directors of the class above them, was that they differed from cattle in stipulating for seats. With the exception of that provision to suit their weakness, the accommodation extended to them resembled pens, and the seats were emphatically seats of penitence, intended to grind the sitter for his mean pittance payment and absence of aspiration to a higher state. Hard angular wood, a low roof, a shabby square of window aloof, demanding of him to quit the seat he insisted on having, if he would indulge in views of the passing scenery,—such was the furniture of dens where a refinement of castigation was practised on villain poverty by denying leathers to the windows, or else buttons to the leathers, so that the windows had either to be up or down, but refused to shelter and freshen simultaneously.

Dacier selected a compartment occupied by two old women, a mother and babe and little maid, and a labouring man. There he installed her, with an eager look that she would not notice.

'You will want the window down,' he said.

She applied to her fellow-travellers for the permission; and struggling to get the window down, he was irritated to animadvert on 'these carriages' of the benevolent railway Company.

'Do not forget that the wealthy are well treated, or you may be unjust,' said she, to pacify him.

His mouth sharpened its line while he tried arts and energies on the refractory window. She told him to leave it. 'You can't breathe this atmosphere!' he cried, and called to a porter, who did the work, remarking that it was rather stiff.

The door was banged and fastened. Dacier had to hang on the step to see her in the farewell. From the platform he saw the top of her bonnet; and why she should have been guilty of this freak of riding in an unwholesome carriage, tasked his power of guessing. He was too English even to have taken the explanation, for he detested the distinguishing of the races in his country, and could not therefore have comprehended her peculiar tenacity of the sense of injury as long as enthusiasm did not arise to obliterate it. He required a course of lessons in Irish.

Sauntering down the lane, he called at Simon Rofe's cottage, and spoke very kindly to the gamekeeper's wife. That might please Diana. It was all he could do at present.

CHAPTER XXI.
'THE YOUNG MINISTER OF STATE'

Descriptions in the newspapers of the rural funeral of Lord Dannisburgh had the effect of rousing flights of tattlers with a twittering of the disused name of Warwick; our social Gods renewed their combat, and the verdict of the jury was again overhauled, to be attacked and maintained, the carpers replying to the champions that they held to their view of it: as heads of bull-dogs are expected to do when they have got a grip of one. It is a point of muscular honour with them never to relax their hold. They will tell you why:—they formed that opinion from the first. And but for the swearing of a particular witness, upon whom the plaintiff had been taught to rely, the verdict would have been different—to prove their soundness of judgement. They could speak from private positive information of certain damnatory circumstances, derived from authentic sources. Visits of a gentleman to the house of a married lady in the absence of the husband? Oh!—The British Lucretia was very properly not legally at home to the masculine world of that day. She plied her distaff in pure seclusion, meditating on her absent lord; or else a fair proportion of the masculine world, which had not yet, has not yet, 'doubled Cape Turk,' approved her condemnation to the sack.

There was talk in the feminine world, at Lady Wathin's assemblies. The elevation of her husband had extended and deepened her influence on the levels where it reigned before, but without, strange as we may think it now, assisting to her own elevation, much aspired for, to the smooth and lively upper pavement of Society, above its tumbled strata. She was near that distinguished surface, not on it. Her circle was practically the same as it was previous to the coveted nominal rank enabling her to trample on those beneath it. And women like that Mrs. Warwick, a woman of no birth, no money, not even honest character, enjoyed the entry undisputed, circulated among the highest:—because people took her rattle for wit!—and because also our nobility, Lady Wathin feared, had no due regard for morality. Our aristocracy, brilliant and ancient though it was, merited rebuke. She grew severe upon aristocratic scandals, whereof were plenty among the frolicsome host just overhead, as vexatious as the drawing-room party to the lodger in the floor below, who has not received an invitation to partake of the festivities and is required to digest the noise. But if ambition is oversensitive, moral indignation is ever consolatory, for it plants us on the Judgement Seat. There indeed we may, sitting with the very Highest, forget our personal disappointments in dispensing reprobation for misconduct, however eminent the offenders.

She was Lady Wathin, and once on an afternoon's call to see poor Lady Dunstane at her town-house, she had been introduced to Lady Pennon, a patroness of Mrs. Warwick, and had met a snub—an icy check-bow of the aristocratic head from the top of the spinal column, and not a word, not a look; the half-turn of a head devoid of mouth and eyes! She practised that forbidding checkbow herself to perfection, so the endurance of it was horrible. A noli me tangere, her husband termed it, in his ridiculous equanimity; and he might term it what he pleased—it was insulting. The solace she had was in hearing that hideous Radical Revolutionary things were openly spoken at Mrs. Warwick's evenings with her friends:—impudently named 'the elect of London.' Pleasing to reflect upon Mrs. Warwick as undermining her supporters, to bring them some day down with a crash! Her 'elect of London' were a queer gathering, by report of them! And Mr. Whitmonby too, no doubt a celebrity, was the right-hand man at these dinner-parties of Mrs. Warwick. Where will not men go to be flattered by a pretty woman! He had declined repeated, successive invitations to Lady Wathin's table. But there of course he would not have had 'the freedom': that is, she rejoiced in thinking defensively and offensively, a moral wall enclosed her topics. The Hon. Percy Dacier had been brought to her Thursday afternoon by. Mr. Quintin Manx, and he had one day dined with her; and he knew Mrs. Warwick—a little, he said. The opportunity was not lost to convey to him, entirely in the interest of sweet Constance Asper, that the moral world entertained a settled view of the very clever woman Mrs. Warwick certainly was. He had asked Diana, on their morning walk to the station, whether she had an enemy: so prone are men, educated by the Drama and Fiction in the belief that the garden of civilized life must be at the mercy of the old wild devourers, to fancy 'villain whispers' an indication of direct animosity. Lady Wathin had no sentiment of the kind.

But she had become acquainted with the other side of the famous Dannisburgh case—the unfortunate plaintiff; and compassion as well as morality moved her to put on a speaking air when Mr. Warwick's name was mentioned. She pictured him to the ladies of her circle as 'one of our true gentlemen in his deportment and his feelings.' He was, she would venture to say, her ideal of an English gentleman. 'But now,' she added commiseratingly, 'ruined; ruined in his health and in his prospects.' A lady inquired if it was the verdict that had thus affected him. Lady Wathin's answer was reported over moral, or substratum, London: 'He is the victim of a fatal passion for his wife; and would take her back to- morrow were she to solicit his forgiveness.' Morality had something to say against this active marital charity, attributable, it was to be feared, to weakness of character on the part of the husband. Still Mrs. Warwick undoubtedly was one of those women (of Satanic construction) who have the art of enslaving the men unhappy enough to cross their path. The nature of the art was hinted, with the delicacy of dainty feet which have to tread in mire to get to safety. Men, alas! are snared in this way. Instances too numerous for the good repute of the swinish sex, were cited, and the question of how Morality was defensible from their grossness passed without a tactical reply. There is no defence: Those women come like the Cholera Morbus—and owing to similar causes. They will prevail until the ideas of men regarding women are purified. Nevertheless the husband who could forgive, even propose to forgive, was deemed by consent generous, however weak. Though she might not have been wholly guilty, she had bitterly offended. And he despatched an emissary to her?—The theme, one may, in their language, 'fear,' was relished as a sugared acid. It was renewed in the late Autumn of the year, when ANTONIA published her new book, entitled THE YOUNG MINISTER of STATE. The signature of the authoress was now known; and from this resurgence of her name in public, suddenly a radiation of tongues from the circle of Lady Wathin declared that the repentant Mrs. Warwick had gone back to her husband's bosom and forgiveness! The rumour spread in spite of sturdy denials at odd corners, counting the red-hot proposal of Mr. Sullivan Smith to eat his head and boots for breakfast if it was proved correct. It filled a yawn of the Clubs for the afternoon. Soon this wanton rumour was met and stifled by another of more morbific density, heavily charged as that which led the sad Eliza to her pyre.

ANTONIA's hero was easily identified. THE YOUNG MINISTER of STATE could be he only who was now at all her parties, always meeting her; had been spied walking with her daily in the park near her house, on his march down to Westminster during the session; and who positively went to concerts and sat under fiddlers to be near her. It accounted moreover for his treatment of Constance Asper. What effrontery of the authoress, to placard herself with him in a book! The likeness of the hero to Percy Dacier once established became striking to glaringness—a proof of her ability, and more of her audacity; still more of her intention to flatter him up to his perdition. By the things written of him, one would imagine the conversations going on behind the scenes. She had the wiles of a Cleopatra, not without some of the Nilene's experiences. A youthful Antony Dacier would be little likely to escape her toils. And so promising a young man! The sigh, the tear for weeping over his destruction, almost fell, such vivid realizing of the prophesy appeared in its pathetic pronouncement.

This low rumour, or malaria, began blowing in the winter, and did not travel fast; for strangely, there was hardly a breath of it in the atmosphere of Dacier, none in Diana's. It rose from groups not so rapidly and largely mixing, and less quick to kindle; whose crazy sincereness battened on the smallest morsel of fact and collected the fictitious by slow absorption. But as guardians of morality, often doing good duty in their office, they are persistent. When Parliament assembled, Mr. Quintin Manx, a punctual member of the House, if nothing else, arrived in town. He was invited to dine with Lady Wathin. After dinner she spoke to him of the absent Constance, and heard of her being well, and expressed a great rejoicing at that. Whereupon the burly old shipowner frowned and puffed. Constance, he said, had plunged into these new spangle, candle and high singing services; was all for symbols, harps, effigies, what not. Lady Wathin's countenance froze in hearing of it. She led Mr. Quintin to a wall-sofa, and said: 'Surely the dear child must have had a disappointment, for her to have taken to those foolish displays of religion! It is generally a sign.'

'Well, ma'am—my lady—I let girls go their ways in such things. I don't interfere. But it's that fellow, or nobody, with her. She has fixed her girl's mind on him, and if she can't columbine as a bride, she will as a nun. Young people must be at some harlequinade.'

'But it is very shocking. And he?'

'He plays last and loose, warm and cold. I'm ready to settle twenty times a nobleman's dowry on my niece and she's a fine girl, a handsome girl, educated up to the brim, fit to queen it in any drawing-room. He holds her by some arts that don't hold him, it seems. He's all for politics.'

'Constance can scarcely be his dupe so far, I should think.'

'How do you mean?'

'Everything points to one secret of his conduct.'

'A woman?'

Lady Wathin's head shook for her sex's pained affirmative.

Mr. Quintin in the same fashion signified the downright negative. 'The fellow's as cold as a fish.'

'Flattery will do anything. There is, I fear, one.'

'Widow? wife? maid?'

'Married, I regret to say.'

'Well, if he'd get over with it,' said Quintin, in whose notions the seductiveness of a married woman could be only temporary, for all the reasons pertaining to her state. At the same time his view of Percy Dacier was changed in thinking it possible that a woman could divert him from his political and social interests. He looked incredulous.

'You have heard of a Mrs. Warwick?' said Lady Wathin.

'Warwick! I have. I've never seen her. At my broker's in the City yesterday I saw the name on a Memorandum of purchase of Shares in a concern promising ten per cent., and not likely to carry the per annum into the plural. He told me she was a grand kind of woman, past advising.'

'For what amount'

'Some thousands, I think it was.'

'She has no money': Lady Wathin corrected her emphasis: 'or ought to have none.'

'She can't have got it from him.'

'Did you notice her Christian name?'

'I don't recollect it, if I did. I thought the woman a donkey.'

'Would you consider me a busybody were I to try to mitigate this woman's evil influence? I love dear Constance, and should be happy to serve her.'

'I want my girl married,' said old Quintin. 'He's one of my Parliamentary chiefs, with first-rate prospects; good family, good sober fellow—at least I thought so; by nature, I mean; barring your incantations. He suits me, she liking him.'

'She admires him, I am sure.'

'She's dead on end for the fellow!'

Lady Wathin felt herself empowered by Quintin Manx to undertake the release of sweet Constance Asper's knight from the toils of his enchantress. For this purpose she had first an interview with Mr. Warwick, and next she hurried to Lady Dunstane at Copsley. There, after jumbling Mr. Warwick's connubial dispositions and Mrs. Warwick's last book, and Mr. Percy Dacier's engagement to the great heiress in a gossipy hotch-potch, she contrived to gather a few items of fact, as that THE YOUNG MINISTER was probably modelled upon Mr. Percy Dacier. Lady Dunstane made no concealment of it as soon as she grew sensible of the angling. But she refused her help to any reconciliation between Mr. and Mrs. Warwick. She declined to listen to Lady Wathin's entreaties. She declined to give her reasons.—These bookworm women, whose pride it is to fancy that they can think for themselves, have a great deal of the heathen in them, as morality discovers when it wears the enlistment ribands and applies yo them to win recruits for a service under the direct blessing of Providence.

Lady Wathin left some darts behind her, in the form of moral exclamations; and really intended morally. For though she did not like Mrs. Warwick, she had no wish to wound, other than by stopping her further studies of the Young Minister, and conducting him to the young lady loving him, besides restoring a bereft husband to his own. How sadly pale and worn poor Mr. Warwick appeared? The portrayal of his withered visage to Lady Dunstane had quite failed to gain a show of sympathy. And so it is ever with your book-worm women pretending to be philosophical! You sound them vainly for a manifestation of the commonest human sensibilities, They turn over the leaves of a Latin book on their laps while you are supplicating them to assist in a work of charity!'

Lady Wathin's interjectory notes haunted Emma's ear. Yet she had seen nothing in Tony to let her suppose that there was trouble of her heart below the surface; and her Tony when she came to Copsley shone in the mood of the day of Lord Dannisburgh's drive down from London with her. She was running on a fresh work; talked of composition as a trifle.

'I suppose the YOUNG MINISTER is Mr. Percy Dacier?' said Emma.

'Between ourselves he is,' Diana replied, smiling at a secret guessed. 'You know my model and can judge of the likeness.'

'You write admiringly of him, Tony.'

'And I do admire him. So would you, Emmy, if you knew him as well as I do now. He pairs with Mr. Redworth; he also is the friend of women. But he lifts us to rather a higher level of intellectual friendship. When the ice has melted—and it is thick at first—he pours forth all his ideas without reserve; and they are deep and noble. Ever since Lord Dannisburgh's death and our sitting together, we have been warm friends —intimate, I would say, if it could be said of one so self-contained. In that respect, no young man was ever comparable with him. And I am encouraged to flatter myself that he unbends to me more than to others.'

'He is engaged, or partly, I hear; why does he not marry?'

'I wish he would!' Diana said, with a most brilliant candour of aspect.

Emma read in it, that it would complete her happiness, possibly by fortifying her sense of security; and that seemed right. Her own meditations, illumined by the beautiful face in her presence, referred to the security of Mr. Dacier.

'So, then, life is going smoothly,' said Emma.

'Yes, at a good pace and smoothly: not a torrent—Thames-like, "without o'erflowing full." It is not Lugano and the Salvatore. Perhaps it is better: as action is better than musing.'

'No troubles whatever?'

'None. Well, except an "adorer" at times. I have to take him as my portion. An impassioned Caledonian has a little bothered me. I met him at Lady Pennon's, and have been meeting him, as soon as I put foot out of my house, ever since. If I could impress and impound him to marry Mary Paynham, I should be glad. By the way, I have consented to let her try at a portrait of me. No, I have no troubles. I have friends, the choicest of the nation; I have health, a field for labour, fairish success with it; a mind alive, such as it is. I feel like that midsummer morning of our last drive out together, the sun high, clearish, clouded enough to be cool. And still I envy Emmy on her sofa, mastering Latin, biting at Greek. What a wise recommendation that was of Mr. Redworth's! He works well in the House. He spoke excellently the other night.'

'He runs over to Ireland this Easter.'

'He sees for himself, and speaks with authority. He sees and feels. Englishmen mean well, but they require an extremity of misery to waken their feelings.'

'It is coming, he says; and absit omen!'

'Mr. Dacier says he is the one Englishman who may always be sure of an Irish hearing; and he does not cajole them, you know. But the English defect is really not want of feeling so much as want of foresight. They will not look ahead. A famine ceasing, a rebellion crushed, they jog on as before, with their Dobbin trot and blinker confidence in "Saxon energy." They should study the Irish: I think it was Mr. Redworth who compared the governing of the Irish to the management of a horse: the rider should not grow restive when the steed begins to kick: calmer; firm, calm, persuasive.'

'Does Mr. Dacier agree?'

'Not always. He has the inveterate national belief that Celtic blood is childish, and the consequently illogical disregard of its hold of impressions. The Irish—for I have them in my heart, though I have not been among them for long at a time—must love you to serve you, and will hate you if you have done them injury and they have not wiped it out— they with a treble revenge, or you with cordial benefits. I have told him so again and again: ventured to suggest measures.'

'He listens to you, Tony?'

'He says I have brains. It ends in a compliment.'

'You have inspired Mr. Redworth.'

'If I have, I have lived for some good.'

Altogether her Tony's conversation proved to Emma that her perusal of the model of THE YOUNG MINISTER OF STATE was an artist's, free, open, and not discoloured by the personal tincture. Her heart plainly was free and undisturbed. She had the same girl's love of her walks where wildflowers grew; if possible, a keener pleasure. She hummed of her happiness in being at Copsley, singing her Planxty Kelly and The Puritani by turns. She stood on land: she was not on the seas. Emma thought so with good reason.

She stood on land, it was true, but she stood on a cliff of the land, the seas below and about her; and she was enabled to hoodwink her friend because the assured sensation of her firm footing deceived her own soul, even while it took short flights to the troubled waters. Of her firm footing she was exultingly proud. She stood high, close to danger, without giddiness. If at intervals her soul flew out like lightning from the rift (a mere shot of involuntary fancy, it seemed to her), the suspicion of instability made her draw on her treasury of impressions of the mornings at Lugano—her loftiest, purest, dearest; and these reinforced her. She did not ask herself why she should have to seek them for aid. In other respects her mind was alert and held no sly covers, as the fiction of a perfect ignorant innocence combined with common intelligence would have us to suppose that the minds of women can do. She was honest as long as she was not directly questioned, pierced to the innermost and sanctum of the bosom. She could honestly summon bright light to her eyes in wishing the man were married. She did not ask herself why she called it up. The remorseless progressive interrogations of a Jesuit Father in pursuit of the bosom's verity might have transfixed it and shown her to herself even then a tossing vessel as to the spirit, far away from that firm land she trod so bravely.

Descending from the woody heights upon London, Diana would have said that her only anxiety concerned young Mr. Arthur Rhodes, whose position she considered precarious, and who had recently taken a drubbing for venturing to show a peep of his head, like an early crocus, in the literary market. Her ANTONIA'S last book had been reviewed obediently to smart taps from the then commanding baton of Mr. Tonans, and Mr. Whitmonby's choice picking of specimens down three columns of his paper. A Literary Review (Charles Rainer's property) had suggested that perhaps 'the talented authoress might be writing too rapidly'; and another, actuated by the public taste of the period for our 'vigorous homely Saxon' in one and two syllable words, had complained of a 'tendency to polysyllabic phraseology.' The remainder, a full majority, had sounded eulogy with all their band-instruments, drum, trumpet, fife, trombone. Her foregoing work had raised her to Fame, which is the Court of a Queen when the lady has beauty and social influence, and critics are her dedicated courtiers, gaping for the royal mouth to be opened, and reserving the kicks of their independent manhood for infamous outsiders, whom they hoist in the style and particular service of pitchforks. They had fallen upon a little volume of verse, 'like a body of barn-door hens on a stranger chick,' Diana complained; and she chid herself angrily for letting it escape her forethought to propitiate them on the author's behalf. Young Rhodes was left with scarce a feather; and what remained to him appeared a preposterous ornament for the decoration of a shivering and welted poet. He laughed, or tried the mouth of laughter. ANTONIA's literary conscience was vexed at the different treatment she had met and so imperatively needed that the reverse of it would have threatened the smooth sailing of her costly household. A merry-go-round of creditors required a corresponding whirligig of receipts.

She felt mercenary, debased by comparison with the well-scourged verse-mason, Orpheus of the untenanted city, who had done his publishing ingenuously for glory: a good instance of the comic-pathetic. She wrote to Emma, begging her to take him in at Copsley for a few days: 'I told you I had no troubles. I am really troubled about this poor boy. He has very little money and has embarked on literature. I cannot induce any of my friends to lend him a hand. Mr. Redworth gruffly insists on his going back to his law-clerk's office and stool, and Mr. Dacier says that no place is vacant. The reality of Lord Dannisburgh's death is brought before me by my helplessness. He would have made him an assistant private Secretary, pending a Government appointment, rather than let me plead in vain.'

Mr. Rhodes with his travelling bag was packed off to Copsley, to enjoy a change of scene after his run of the gauntlet. He was very heartily welcomed by Lady Dunstane, both for her Tony's sake and his own modest worship of that luminary, which could permit of being transparent; but chiefly she welcomed him as the living proof of Tony's disengagement from anxiety, since he was her one spot of trouble, and could easily be comforted by reading with her, and wandering through the Spring woods along the heights. He had a happy time, midway in air between his accomplished hostess and his protecting Goddess. His bruises were soon healed. Each day was radiant to him, whether it rained or shone; and by his looks and what he said of himself Lady Dunstane understood that he was in the highest temper of the human creature tuned to thrilling accord with nature. It was her generous Tony's work. She blessed it, and liked the youth the better.

During the stay of Mr. Arthur Rhodes at Copsley, Sir Lukin came on a visit to his wife. He mentioned reports in the scandal-papers: one, that Mr. P. D. would shortly lead to the altar the lovely heiress Miss A., Percy Dacier and Constance Asper:—another, that a reconciliation was to be expected between the beautiful authoress Mrs. W. and her husband. 'Perhaps it's the best thing she can do,' Sir Lukin added.

Lady Dunstane pronounced a woman's unforgiving: 'Never.' The revolt of her own sensations assured her of Tony's unconquerable repugnance. In conversation subsequently with Arthur Rhodes, she heard that he knew the son of Mr. Warwick's attorney, a Mr. Fern; and he had gathered from him some information of Mr. Warwick's condition of health. It had been alarming; young Fern said it was confirmed heart-disease. His father frequently saw Mr. Warwick, and said he was fretting himself to death.

It seemed just a possibility that Tony's natural compassionateness had wrought on her to immolate herself and nurse to his end the man who had wrecked her life. Lady Dunstane waited for the news. At last she wrote, touching the report incidentally. There was no reply. The silence ensuing after such a question responded forcibly.

CHAPTER XXII.
BETWEEN DIANA AND DACIER: THE WIND EAST OVER BLEAK LAND

On the third day of the Easter recess Percy Dacier landed from the Havre steamer at Caen and drove straightway for the sandy coast, past fields of colza to brine-blown meadows of coarse grass, and then to the low dunes and long stretching sands of the ebb in semicircle: a desolate place at that season; with a dwarf fishing-village by the shore; an East wind driving landward in streamers every object that had a scrap to fly. He made head to the inn, where the first person he encountered in the passage was Diana's maid Danvers, who relaxed from the dramatic exaggeration of her surprise at the sight of a real English gentleman in these woebegone regions, to inform him that her mistress might be found walking somewhere along the sea-shore, and had her dog to protect her. They were to stay here a whole week, Danvers added, for a conveyance of her private sentiments. Second thoughts however whispered to her shrewdness that his arrival could only be by appointment. She had been anticipating something of the sort for some time.

Dacier butted against the stringing wind, that kept him at a rocking incline to his left for a mile. He then discerned in what had seemed a dredger's dot on the sands, a lady's figure, unmistakably she, without the corroborating testimony of Leander paw-deep in the low-tide water. She was out at a distance on the ebb-sands, hurtled, gyred, beaten to all shapes, in rolls, twists, volumes, like a blown banner-flag, by the pressing wind. A kerchief tied her bonnet under her chin. Bonnet and breast-ribands rattled rapidly as drummer-sticks. She stood near the little running ripple of the flat sea-water, as it hurried from a long streaked back to a tiny imitation of spray. When she turned to the shore she saw him advancing, but did not recognize;

when they met she merely looked with wide parted lips. This was no appointment.

'I had to see you,' Dacier said.

She coloured to a deeper red than the rose-conjuring wind had whipped in her cheeks. Her quick intuition of the reason of his coming barred a mental evasion, and she had no thought of asking either him or herself what special urgency had brought him.

'I have been here four days.'

'Lady Esquart spoke of the place.'

'Lady Esquart should not have betrayed me.'

'She did it inadvertently, without an idea of my profiting by it.'

Diana indicated the scene in a glance. 'Dreary country, do you think?'

'Anywhere!'—said he.

They walked up the sand-heap. The roaring Easter with its shrieks and whistles at her ribands was not favourable to speech. His 'Anywhere!' had a penetrating significance, the fuller for the break that left it vague.

Speech between them was commanded; he could not be suffered to remain. She descended upon a sheltered pathway running along a ditch, the border of pastures where cattle cropped, raised heads, and resumed their one comforting occupation.

Diana gazed on them, smarting from the buffets of the wind she had met.

'No play of their tails to-day'; she said, as she slackened her steps. 'You left Lady Esquart well?'

'Lady Esquart . . . I think was well. I had to see you. I thought you would be with her in Berkshire. She told me of a little sea-side place close to Caen.'

'You had to see me?'

'I miss you now if it's a day!'

'I heard a story in London . . .'

'In London there are many stories. I heard one. Is there a foundation for it?'

'No.'

He breathed relieved. 'I wanted to see you once before . . . if it was true. It would have made a change in my life-a gap.'

'You do me the honour to like my Sunday evenings?'

'Beyond everything London can offer.'

'A letter would have reached me.'

'I should have had to wait for the answer. There is no truth in it?'

Her choice was to treat the direct assailant frankly or imperil her defence by the ordinary feminine evolutions, which might be taken for inviting: poor pranks always.

'There have been overtures,' she said.

'Forgive me; I have scarcely the right to ask . . . speak of it.!

'My friends may use their right to take an interest in my fortunes.'

'I thought I might, on my way to Paris, turn aside . . . coming by this route.'

'If you determined not to lose much of your time.'

The coolness of her fencing disconcerted a gentleman conscious of his madness. She took instant advantage of any circuitous move; she gave him no practicable point. He was little skilled in the arts of attack, and felt that she checked his impetuousness; respected her for it, chafed at it, writhed with the fervours precipitating him here, and relapsed on his pleasure in seeing her face, hearing her voice.

'Your happiness, I hope, is the chief thought in such a case,' he said.

'I am sure you would consider it.'

'I can't quite forget my own.'

'You compliment an ambitious hostess.'

Dacier glanced across the pastures, 'What was it that tempted you to this place?'

'A poet would say it looks like a figure in the shroud. It has no features; it has a sort of grandeur belonging to death. I heard of it as the place where I might be certain of not meeting an acquaintance.'

'And I am the intruder.'

'An hour or two will not give you that title.'

'Am I to count the minutes by my watch?'

'By the sun. We will supply you an omelette and piquette, and send you back sobered and friarly—to Caen for Paris at sunset.'

'Let the fare be Spartan. I could take my black broth with philosophy every day of the year under your auspices. What I should miss . . .'

'You bring no news of the world or the House?'

'None. You know as much as I know. The Irish agitation is chronic. The Corn-law threatens to be the same.'

'And your Chief—in personal colloquy?'

'He keeps a calm front. I may tell you: there is nothing I would not confide to you: he has let fall some dubious words in private. I don't know what to think of them.'

'But if he should waver?'

'It's not wavering. It's the openness of his mind.'

'Ah! the mind. We imagine it free. The House and the country are the sentient frame governing the mind of the politician more than his ideas. He cannot think independently of them:—nor I of my natural anatomy. You will test the truth of that after your omelette and piquette, and marvel at the quitting of your line of route for Paris. As soon as the mind attempts to think independently, it is like a kite with the cord cut, and performs a series of darts and frisks, that have the look of wildest liberty till you see it fall flat to earth. The openness of his mind is most honourable to him.'

'Ominous for his party.'

'Likely to be good for his country.'

'That is the question.'

'Prepare to encounter it. In politics I am with the active minority on behalf of the inert but suffering majority. That is my rule. It leads, unless you have a despotism, to the conquering side. It is always the noblest. I won't say, listen to me; only do believe my words have some weight. This is a question of bread.'

'It involves many other questions.'

'And how clearly those leaders put their case! They are admirable debaters. If I were asked to write against them, I should have but to quote them to confound my argument. I tried it once, and wasted a couple of my precious hours.'

'They are cogent debaters,' Dacier assented. 'They make me wince now and then, without convincing me: I own it to you. The confession is not agreeable, though it's a small matter.'

'One's pride may feel a touch with the foils as keenly as the point of a rapier,' said Diana.

The remark drew a sharp look of pleasure from him.

'Does the Princess Egeria propose to dismiss the individual she inspires, when he is growing most sensible of her wisdom?'

'A young Minister of State should be gleaning at large when holiday is granted him.'

Dacier coloured. 'May I presume on what is currently reported?'

'Parts, parts; a bit here, a bit there,' she rejoined. 'Authors find their models where they can, and generally hit on the nearest.'

'Happy the nearest!'

'If you run to interjections I shall cite you a sentence, from your latest speech in the House.'

He asked for it, and to school him she consented to flatter with her recollection of his commonest words:

'"Dealing with subjects of this nature emotionally does, not advance us a calculable inch."'

'I must have said that in relation to hard matter of business.'

'It applies. There is my hostelry, and the spectral form of Danvers, utterly depaysee. Have you spoken to the poor soul? I can never discover the links of her attachment to my service.'

'She knows a good mistress.—I have but a few minutes, if you are relentless. May I . . ., shall I ever be privileged to speak your Christian name?'

'My Christian name! It is Pagan. In one sphere I am Hecate. Remember that.'

'I am not among the people who so regard you.'

'The time may come.'

'Diana!'

'Constance!'

'I break no tie. I owe no allegiance whatever to the name.'

'Keep to the formal title with me. We are Mrs. Warwick and Mr. Dacier. I think I am two years younger than you; socially therefore ten in seniority; and I know how this flower of friendship is nourished and may be withered. You see already what you have done? You have cast me on the discretion of my maid. I suppose her trusty, but I am at her mercy, and a breath from her to the people beholding me as Hecate queen of Witches! . . . I have a sensation of the scirocco it would blow.'

'In that event, the least I can offer is my whole life.'

'We will not conjecture the event.'

'The best I could hope for!'

'I see I shall have to revise the next edition of THE YOUNG MINISTER, and make an emotional curate of him. Observe Danvers. The woman is wretched; and now she sees me coming she pretends to be using her wits in studying the things about her, as I have directed. She is a riddle. I have the idea that any morning she may explode; and yet I trust her and sleep soundly. I must be free, though I vex the world's watchdogs.—So, Danvers, you are noticing how thoroughly Frenchwomen do their work.'

Danvers replied with a slight mincing: 'They may, ma'am; but they chatter chatter so.'

'The result proves that it is not a waste of energy. They manage their fowls too.'

'They've no such thing as mutton, ma'am.'

Dacier patriotically laughed.

'She strikes the apology for wealthy and leisurely landlords,' Diana said.

Danvers remarked that the poor fed meagrely in France. She was not convinced of its being good for them by hearing that they could work on it sixteen hours out of the four and twenty.

Mr. Percy Dacier's repast was furnished to him half an hour later. At sunset Diana, taking Danvers beside her, walked with him to the line of the country road bearing on Caen. The wind had sunk. A large brown disk paused rayless on the western hills.

'A Dacier ought to feel at home in Normandy; and you may have sprung from this neighbourhood,' said she, simply to chat. 'Here the land is poorish, and a mile inland rich enough to bear repeated crops of colza, which tries the soil, I hear. As for beauty, those blue hills you see, enfold charming valleys. I meditate an expedition to Harcourt before I return. An English professor of his native tongue at the Lycee at Caen told me on my way here that for twenty shillings a week you may live in royal ease round about Harcourt. So we have our bed and board in prospect if fortune fails us, Danvers!'

'I would rather die in England, ma'am,' was the maid's reply.

Dacier set foot on his carriage-step. He drew a long breath to say a short farewell, and he and Diana parted.

They parted as the plainest of sincere good friends, each at heart respecting the other for the repression of that which their hearts craved; any word of which might have carried them headlong, bound together on a Mazeppa-race, with scandal for the hounding wolves, and social ruin for the rocks and torrents.

Dacier was the thankfuller, the most admiring of the two; at the same time the least satisfied. He saw the abyss she had aided him in escaping; and it was refreshful to look abroad after his desperate impulse. Prominent as he stood before the world, he could not think without a shudder of behaving like a young frenetic of the passion. Those whose aim is at the leadership of the English people know, that however truly based the charges of hypocrisy, soundness of moral fibre runs throughout the country and is the national integrity, which may condone old sins for present service; but will not have present sins to flout it. He was in tune with the English character. The passion was in him nevertheless, and the stronger for a slow growth that confirmed its union of the mind and heart. Her counsel fortified him, her suggestions opened springs; her phrases were golden-lettered in his memory; and more, she had worked an extraordinary change in his views of life and aptitude for social converse: he acknowledged it with genial candour. Through her he was encouraged, led, excited to sparkle with the witty, feel new gifts, or a greater breadth of nature; and thanking her, he became thirstily susceptible to her dark beauty; he claimed to have found the key of her, and he prized it. She was not passionless: the blood flowed warm. Proud, chaste, she was nobly spirited; having an intellectual refuge from the besiegings of the blood; a rockfortress. The 'wife no wife' appeared to him, striking the higher elements of the man, the commonly masculine also.—Would he espouse her, had he the chance?— to-morrow! this instant! With her to back him, he would be doubled in manhood, doubled in brain and heart-energy. To call her wife, spring from her and return, a man might accept his fate to fight Trojan or Greek, sure of his mark on the enemy.

But if, after all, this imputed Helen of a decayed Paris passed, submissive to the legitimate solicitor, back to her husband?

The thought shot Dacier on his legs for a look at the blank behind him. He vowed she had promised it should not be. Could it ever be, after the ruin the meanly suspicious fellow had brought upon her?— Diana voluntarily reunited to the treacherous cur?

He sat, resolving sombrely that if the debate arose he would try what force he had to save her from such an ignominy, and dedicate his life to her, let the world wag its tongue. So the knot would be cut.

Men unaccustomed to a knot in their system find the prospect of cutting it an extreme relief, even when they know that the cut has an edge to wound mortally as well as pacify. The wound was not heavy payment for the rapture of having so incomparable a woman his own. He reflected wonderingly on the husband, as he had previously done, and came again to the conclusion that it was a poor creature, abjectly jealous of a wife, he could neither master, nor equal, nor attract. And thinking of jealousy, Dacier felt none; none of individuals, only of facts: her marriage, her bondage. Her condemnation to perpetual widowhood angered him, as at an unrighteous decree. The sharp sweet bloom of her beauty, fresh in swarthiness, under the whipping Easter, cried out against that loathed inhumanity. Or he made it cry.

Being a stranger to the jealousy of men, he took the soft assurance that he was preferred above them all. Competitors were numerous: not any won her eyes as he did. She revealed nothing of the same pleasures in the shining of the others touched by her magical wand. Would she have pardoned one of them the 'Diana!' bursting from his mouth?

She was not a woman for trifling, still less for secresy. He was as little the kind of lover. Both would be ready to take up their burden, if the burden was laid on them. Diana had thus far impressed him.

Meanwhile he faced the cathedral towers of the ancient Norman city, standing up in the smoky hues of the West; and a sentence out of her book seemed fitting to the scene and what he felt. He rolled it over luxuriously as the next of delights to having her beside him.—She wrote of; 'Thoughts that are bare dark outlines, coloured by some odd passion of the soul, like towers of a distant city seen in the funeral waste of day.'—His bluff English anti-poetic training would have caused him to shrug at the stuff coming from another pen: he might condescendingly have criticized it, with a sneer embalmed in humour. The words were hers; she had written them; almost by a sort of anticipation, he imagined; for he at once fell into the mood they suggested, and had a full crop of the 'bare dark outlines' of thoughts coloured by his particular form of passion.

Diana had impressed him powerfully when she set him swallowing and assimilating a sentence ethereally thin in substance of mere sentimental significance, that he would antecedently have read aloud in a drawing-room, picking up the book by hazard, as your modern specimen of romantic vapouring. Mr. Dacier however was at the time in observation of the towers of Caen, fresh from her presence, animated to some conception of her spirit. He drove into the streets, desiring, half determining, to risk a drive back on the morrow.

The cold light of the morrow combined with his fear of distressing her to restrain him. Perhaps he thought it well not to risk his gains. He was a northerner in blood. He may have thought it well not further to run the personal risk immediately.

CHAPTER XXIII.
RECORDS A VISIT TO DIANA FROM ONE OF THE WORLD'S GOOD WOMEN

Pure disengagement of contemplativeness had selected. Percy Dacier as the model of her YOUNG MINISTER OF STATE, Diana supposed. Could she otherwise have dared to sketch him? She certainly would not have done it now.

That was a reflection similar to what is entertained by one who has dropped from a precipice to the midway ledge over the abyss, where caution of the whole sensitive being is required for simple self-preservation. How could she have been induced to study and portray him! It seemed a form of dementia.

She thought this while imagining the world to be interrogating her. When she interrogated herself, she flew to Lugano and her celestial Salvatore, that she might be defended from a charge of the dreadful weakness of her sex. Surely she there had proof of her capacity for pure disengagement. Even in recollection the springs of spiritual happiness renewed the bubbling crystal play. She believed that a divineness had wakened in her there, to strengthen her to the end, ward her from any complicity in her sex's culprit blushing.

Dacier's cry of her name was the cause, she chose to think, of the excessive circumspection she must henceforth practise; precariously footing, embracing hardest earth, the plainest rules, to get back to safety. Not that she was personally endangered, or at least not spiritually; she could always fly in soul to her heights. But she had now to be on guard, constantly in the fencing attitude. And watchful of herself as well. That was admitted with a ready frankness, to save it from being a necessitated and painful confession: for the voluntary-acquiescence, if it involved her in her sex, claimed an individual exemption. 'Women are women, and I am a woman but I am I, and unlike them: I see we are weak, and weakness tempts: in owning the prudence of guarded steps, I am armed. It is by dissembling, feigning immunity, that we are imperilled.' She would have phrased it so, with some anger at her feminine nature as well as at the subjection forced on her by circumstances.

Besides, her position and Percy Dacier's threw the fancied danger into remoteness. The world was her stepmother, vigilant to become her judge; and the world was his taskmaster, hopeful of him, yet able to strike him down for an offence. She saw their situation as he did. The course of folly must be bravely taken, if taken at all: Disguise degraded her to the reptiles.

This was faced. Consequently there was no fear of it.

She had very easily proved that she had skill and self-possession to keep him rational, and therefore they could continue to meet. A little outburst of frenzy to a reputably handsome woman could be treated as the froth of a passing wave. Men have the trick, infants their fevers.

Diana's days were spent in reasoning. Her nights were not so tuneable to the superior mind. When asleep she was the sport of elves that danced her into tangles too deliciously unravelled, and left new problems for the wise-eyed and anxious morning. She solved them with the thought that in sleep it was the mere ordinary woman who fell a prey to her tormentors; awake, she dispersed the swarm, her sky was clear. Gradually the persecution ceased, thanks to her active pen.

A letter from her legal adviser, old Mr. Braddock, informed her that no grounds existed for apprehending marital annoyance, and late in May her household had resumed its customary round.

She examined her accounts. The Debit and Credit sides presented much of the appearance of male and female in our jog-trot civilization. They matched middling well; with rather too marked a tendency to strain the leash and run frolic on the part of friend Debit (the wanton male), which deepened the blush of the comparison. Her father had noticed the same funny thing in his effort to balance his tugging accounts: 'Now then for a look at Man and Wife': except that he made Debit stand for the portly frisky female, Credit the decorous and contracted other half, a prim gentleman of a constitutionally lean habit of body, remonstrating with her. 'You seem to forget that we are married, my dear, and must walk in step or bundle into the Bench,' Dan Merion used to say.

Diana had not so much to rebuke in Mr. Debit; or not at the first reckoning. But his ways were curious. She grew distrustful of him, after dismissing him with a quiet admonition and discovering a series of ambush bills, which he must have been aware of when he was allowed to pass as an honourable citizen. His answer to her reproaches pleaded the necessitousness of his purchases and expenditure: a capital plea; and Mrs. Credit was requested by him, in a courteous manner, to drive her pen the faster, so that she might wax to a corresponding size and satisfy the world's idea of fitness in couples. She would have costly furniture, because it pleased her taste; and a French cook, for a like reason, in justice to her guests; and trained servants; and her tribe of pensioners; flowers she would have profuse and fresh at her windows and over the rooms; and the pictures and engravings on the walls were (always for the good reason mentioned) choice ones; and she had a love of old lace, she loved colours as she loved cheerfulness, and silks, and satin hangings, Indian ivory carvings, countless mirrors, Oriental woods, chairs and desks with some feature or a flourish in them, delicate tables with antelope legs, of approved workmanship in the chronology of European upholstery, and marble clocks of cunning device to symbol Time, mantelpiece decorations, illustrated editions of her favourite authors; her bed-chambers, too, gave the nest for sleep a dainty cosiness in aerial draperies. Hence, more or less directly, the peccant bills. Credit was reduced to reckon to a nicety the amount she could rely on positively: her fixed income from her investments and the letting of The Crossways: the days of half-yearly payments that would magnify her to some proportions beside the alarming growth of her partner, who was proud of it, and referred her to the treasures she could summon with her pen, at a murmur of dissatisfaction. His compliments were sincere; they were seductive. He assured her that she had struck a rich vein in an inexhaustible mine; by writing only a very little faster she could double her income; counting a broader popularity, treble it; and so on a tide of success down the widening river to a sea sheer golden. Behold how it sparkles! Are we then to stint our winged hours of youth for want of courage to realize the riches we can command? Debit was eloquent, he was unanswerable.

Another calculator, an accustomed and lamentably-scrupulous arithmetician, had been at work for some time upon a speculative summing of the outlay of Diana's establishment, as to its chances of swamping the income. Redworth could guess pretty closely the cost of a house hold, if his care for the holder set him venturing on aver ages. He knew nothing of her ten per cent. investment and considered her fixed income a beggarly regiment to marshal against the invader. He fancied however, in his ignorance of literary profits, that a popular writer, selling several editions, had come to an El Dorado. There was the mine. It required a diligent worker. Diana was often struck by hearing Redworth ask her when her next book might be expected. He appeared to have an eagerness in hurrying her to produce, and she had to say that she was not a nimble writer. His flattering impatience was vexatious. He admired her work, yet he did his utmost to render it little admirable. His literary taste was not that of young Arthur Rhodes, to whom she could read her chapters, appearing to take counsel upon them while drinking the eulogies: she suspected him of prosaic ally wishing her to make money, and though her exchequer was beginning to know the need of it, the author's lofty mind disdained such sordidness: to be excused, possibly, for a failing productive energy. She encountered obstacles to imaginative composition. With the pen in her hand, she would fall into heavy musings; break a sentence to muse, and not on the subject. She slept unevenly at night, was drowsy by day, unless the open air was about her, or animating friends. Redworth's urgency to get her to publish was particularly annoying when she felt how greatly THE YOUNG MINISTER OF STATE would have been improved had she retained the work to brood over it, polish, re-write passages, perfect it. Her musings embraced long dialogues of that work, never printed; they sprang up, they passed from memory; leaving a distaste for her present work. THE CANTATRICE: far more poetical than the preceding, in the opinion of Arthur Rhodes; and the story was more romantic; modelled on a Prima Donna she had met at the musical parties of Henry Wilmers, after hearing Redworth tell of Charles Rainer's quaint passion for the woman, or the idea of the woman. Diana had courted her, studied and liked her. The picture she was drawing of the amiable and gifted Italian, of her villain Roumanian husband, and of the eccentric, high-minded, devoted Englishman, was good in a fashion; but considering the theme, she had reasonable apprehension that her

CANTATRICE would not repay her for the time and labour bestowed on it. No clever transcripts of the dialogue of the day occurred; no hair-breadth 'scapes, perils by sea and land, heroisms of the hero, fine shrieks of the heroine; no set scenes of catching pathos and humour; no distinguishable points of social satire—equivalent to a smacking of the public on the chaps, which excites it to grin with keen discernment of the author's intention. She did not appeal to the senses nor to a superficial discernment. So she had the anticipatory sense of its failure; and she wrote her best, in perverseness; of course she wrote slowly; she wrote more and more realistically of the characters and the downright human emotions, less of the wooden supernumeraries of her story, labelled for broad guffaw or deluge tears—the grappling natural links between our public and an author. Her feelings were aloof. They flowed at a hint of a scene of THE YOUNG MINISTER. She could not put them into THE CANTATRICE. And Arthur Rhodes pronounced this work poetical beyond its predecessors, for the reason that the chief characters were alive and the reader felt their pulses. He meant to say, they were poetical inasmuch as they were creations.

The slow progress of a work not driven by the author's feelings necessitated frequent consultations between Debit and Credit, resulting in altercations, recriminations, discord of the yoked and divergent couple. To restore them to their proper trot in harness, Diana reluctantly went to her publisher for an advance item of the sum she was to receive, and the act increased her distaste. An idea came that she would soon cease to be able to write at all. What then? Perhaps by selling her invested money, and ultimately The Crossways, she would have enough for her term upon earth. Necessarily she had to think that short, in order to reckon it as nearly enough. 'I am sure,' she said to herself, 'I shall not trouble the world very long.' A strange languor beset her; scarcely melancholy, for she conceived the cheerfulness of life and added to it in company; but a nervelessness, as though she had been left by the stream on the banks, and saw beauty and pleasure sweep along and away, while the sun that primed them dried her veins. At this time she was gaining her widest reputation for brilliancy of wit. Only to welcome guests were her evenings ever spent at home. She had no intimate understanding of the deadly wrestle of the conventional woman with her nature which she was undergoing below the surface. Perplexities she acknowledged, and the prudence of guardedness. 'But as I am sure not to live very long, we may as well meet.' Her meetings with Percy Dacier were therefore hardly shunned; and his behaviour did not warn her to discountenance them. It would have been cruel to exclude him from her select little dinners of eight. Whitmonby, Westlake, Henry Wilmers and the rest, she perhaps aiding, schooled him in the conversational art. She heard it said of him, that the courted discarder of the sex, hitherto a mere politician, was wonderfully humanized. Lady Pennon fell to talking of him hopefully. She declared him to be one of the men who unfold tardily, and only await the mastering passion. If the passion had come, it was controlled. His command of himself melted Diana. How could she forbid his entry to the houses she frequented? She was glad to see him. He showed his pleasure in seeing her. Remembering his tentative indiscretion on those foreign sands, she reflected that he had been easily checked: and the like was not to be said of some others. Beautiful women in her position provoke an intemperateness that contrasts touchingly with the self-restraint of a particular admirer. Her 'impassioned Caledonian' was one of a host, to speak of whom and their fits of lunacy even to her friend Emma, was repulsive. She bore with them, foiled them, passed them, and recovered her equanimity; but the contrast called to her to dwell on it, the self-restraint whispered of a depth of passion....

She was shocked at herself for a singular tremble 'she experienced, without any beating of the heart, on hearing one day that the marriage of Percy Dacier and Miss Asper was at last definitely fixed. Mary Paynham brought her the news. She had it from a lady who had come across Miss Asper at Lady Wathin's assemblies, and considered the great heiress extraordinarily handsome.

'A golden miracle,' Diana gave her words to say. 'Good looks and gold together are rather superhuman. The report may be this time true.' Next afternoon the card of Lady Wathin requested Mrs. Warwick to grant her a private interview.

Lady Wathin, as one of the order of women who can do anything in a holy cause, advanced toward Mrs. Warwick, unabashed by the burden of her mission, and spinally prepared, behind benevolent smilings, to repay dignity of mien with a similar erectness of dignity. They touched fingers and sat. The preliminaries to the matter of the interview were brief between ladies physically sensible of antagonism and mutually too scornful of subterfuges in one another's presence to beat the bush.

Lady Wathin began. 'I am, you are aware, Mrs. Warwick, a cousin of your friend Lady Dunstane.'

'You come to me on business?' Diana said.

'It may be so termed. I have no personal interest in it. I come to lay certain facts before you which I think you should know. We think it better that an acquaintance, and one of your sex, should state the case to you, instead of having recourse to formal intermediaries, lawyers—'

'Lawyers?'

'Well, my husband is a lawyer, it is true. In the course of his professional vocations he became acquainted with Mr. Warwick. We have latterly seen a good deal of him. He is, I regret to say, seriously unwell.'

'I have heard of it.'

'He has no female relations, it appears. He needs more care than he can receive from hirelings.'

'Are you empowered by him, Lady Wathin?'

'I am, Mrs. Warwick. We will not waste time in apologies. He is most anxious for a reconciliation. It seems to Sir Cramborne and to me the most desireable thing for all parties concerned, if you can be induced to regard it in that light. Mr. Warwick may or may not live; but the estrangement is quite undoubtedly the cause of his illness. I touch on nothing connected with it. I simply wish that you should not be in ignorance of his proposal and his condition.'

Diana bowed calmly. 'I grieve at his condition. His proposal has already been made and replied to.'

'Oh, but, Mrs. Warwick, an immediate and decisive refusal of a proposal so fraught with consequences . . . !'

'Ah, but, Lady Wathin, you are now outstepping the limits prescribed by the office you have undertaken.'

'You will not lend ear to an intercession?'

'I will not.'

'Of course, Mrs. Warwick, it is not for me to hint at things that lawyers could say on the subject.'

'Your forbearance is creditable, Lady Wathin.'

'Believe me, Mrs. Warwick, the step is—I speak in my husband's name as well as my own—strongly to be advised.'

'If I hear one word more of it, I leave the country.'

'I should be sorry indeed at any piece of rashness depriving your numerous friends of your society. We have recently become acquainted with Mr. Redworth, and I know the loss you would be to them. I have not attempted an appeal to your feelings, Mrs. Warwick.'

'I thank you warmly, Lady Wathin, for what you have not done.'

The aristocratic airs of Mrs. Warwick were annoying to Lady Wathin when she considered that they were borrowed, and that a pattern morality could regard the woman as ostracized: nor was it agreeable to be looked at through eyelashes under partially lifted brows. She had come to appeal to the feelings of the wife; at any rate, to discover if she had some and was better than a wild adventuress.

'Our life below is short!' she said. To which Diana tacitly assented.

'We have our little term, Mrs. Warwick. It is soon over.'

'On the other hand, the platitudes concerning it are eternal.'

Lady Wathin closed her eyes, that the like effect might be produced on her ears. 'Ah! they are the truths. But it is not my business to preach. Permit me to say that I feel deeply for your husband.'

'I am glad of Mr. Warwick's having friends; and they are many, I hope.'

'They cannot behold him perishing, without an effort on his behalf.'

A chasm of silence intervened. Wifely pity was not sounded in it.

'He will question me, Mrs. Warwick.'

'You can report to him the heads of our conversation, Lady Wathin.'

'Would you—it is your husband's most earnest wish; and our house is open to his wife and to him for the purpose; and it seems to us that . . . indeed it might avert a catastrophe you would necessarily deplore:—would you consent to meet him at my house?'

'It has already been asked, Lady Wathin, and refused.'

'But at my house-under our auspices!'

Diana glanced at the clock. 'Nowhere.'

'Is it not—pardon me—a wife's duty, Mrs. Warwick, at least to listen?'

'Lady Wathin, I have listened to you.'

'In the case of his extreme generosity so putting it, for the present, Mrs. Warwick, that he asks only to be heard personally by his wife! It may preclude so much.'

Diana felt a hot wind across her skin.

She smiled and said: 'Let me thank you for bringing to an end a mission that must have been unpleasant to you.'

'But you will meditate on it, Mrs. Warwick, will you not? Give me that assurance!'

'I shall not forget it,' said Diana.

Again the ladies touched fingers, with an interchange of the social grimace of cordiality. A few words of compassion for poor Lady Dunstane's invalided state covered Lady Wathin's retreat.

She left, it struck her ruffled sentiments, an icy libertine, whom any husband caring for his dignity and comfort was well rid of; and if only she could have contrived allusively to bring in the name of Mr. Percy Dacier, just to show these arrant coquettes, or worse, that they were not quite so privileged to pursue their intrigues obscurely as they imagined, it would have soothed her exasperation.

She left a woman the prey of panic.

Diana thought of Emma and Redworth, and of their foolish interposition to save her character and keep her bound. She might now have been free! The struggle with her manacles reduced her to a state of rebelliousness, from which issued vivid illuminations of the one means of certain escape; an abhorrent hissing cavern, that led to a place named Liberty, her refuge, but a hectic place.

Unable to write, hating the house which held her a fixed mark for these attacks, she had an idea of flying straight to her beloved Lugano lake, and there hiding, abandoning her friends, casting off the slave's name she bore, and living free in spirit. She went so far as to reckon the cost of a small household there, and justify the violent step by an exposition of retrenchment upon her large London expenditure. She had but to say farewell to Emma, no other tie to cut! One morning on the Salvatore heights would wash her clear of the webs defacing and entangling her.

CHAPTER XXIV.
# INDICATES A SOUL PREPARED FOR DESPERATION

The month was August, four days before the closing of Parliament, and Diana fancied it good for Arthur Rhodes to run down with her to Copsley. He came to her invitation joyfully, reminding her of Lady Dunstane's wish to hear some chapters of THE CANTATRICE, and the MS. was packed. They started, taking rail and fly, and winding up the distance on foot. August is the month of sober maturity and majestic foliage, songless, but a crowned and royal-robed queenly month; and the youngster's appreciation of the homely scenery refreshed Diana; his delight in being with her was also pleasant. She had no wish to exchange him for another; and that was a strengthening thought.

At Copsley the arrival of their luggage had prepared the welcome. Warm though it was, Diana perceived a change in Emma, an unwonted reserve, a doubtfulness of her eyes, in spite of tenderness; and thus thrown back on herself, thinking that if she had followed her own counsel (as she called her impulse) in old days, there would have been no such present misery, she at once, and unconsciously, assumed a guarded look. Based on her knowledge of her honest footing, it was a little defiant. Secretly in her bosom it was sharpened to a slight hostility by the knowledge that her mind had been straying. The guilt and the innocence combined to clothe her in mail, the innocence being positive, the guilt so vapoury. But she was armed only if necessary, and there was no requirement for armour. Emma did not question at all. She saw the alteration in her Tony: she was too full of the tragic apprehensiveness, overmastering her to speak of trifles. She had never confided to Tony the exact nature and the growth of her malady, thinking it mortal, and fearing to alarm her dearest.

A portion of the manuscript was read out by Arthur Rhodes in the evening; the remainder next morning. Redworth perceptibly was the model of the English hero; and as to his person, no friend could complain of the sketch; his clear-eyed heartiness, manliness, wholesomeness—a word of Lady Dunstane's regarding him,—and his handsome braced figure, were well painted. Emma forgave the: insistance on a certain bluntness of the nose, in consideration of the fond limning of his honest and expressive eyes, and the 'light on his temples,' which they had noticed together. She could not so easily forgive the realistic picture of the man: an exaggeration, she thought, of small foibles, that even if they existed, should not have been stressed. The turn for 'calculating' was shown up ridiculously; Mr. Cuthbert Dering was calculating in his impassioned moods as well as in his cold. His head was a long division of ciphers. He had statistics for spectacles, and beheld the world through them, and the mistress he worshipped.

'I see,' said Emma, during a pause; 'he is a Saxon. You still affect to have the race en grippe, Tony.'

'I give him every credit for what he is,' Diana replied. 'I admire the finer qualities of the race as much as any one. You want to have them presented to you in enamel, Emmy.'

But the worst was an indication that the mania for calculating in and out of season would lead to the catastrophe destructive of his happiness. Emma could not bear that. Without asking herself whether it could be possible that Tony knew the secret, or whether she would have laid it bare, her sympathy for Redworth revolted at the exposure. She was chilled. She let it pass; she merely said: 'I like the writing.'

Diana understood that her story was condemned.

She put on her robes of philosophy to cloak discouragement. 'I am glad the writing pleases you.'

'The characters are as true as life!' cried Arthur Rhodes. 'The Cantatrice drinking porter from the pewter at the slips after harrowing the hearts of her audience, is dearer to me than if she had tottered to a sofa declining sustenance; and because her creatrix has infused such blood of life into her that you accept naturally whatever she does. She was exhausted, and required the porter, like a labourer in the cornfield.'

Emma looked at him, and perceived the poet swamped by the admirer. Taken in conjunction with Mr. Cuthbert Dering's frenzy for calculating, she disliked the incident of the porter and the pewter.

'While the Cantatrice swallowed her draught, I suppose Mr. Dering counted the cost?' she said.

'It really might be hinted,' said Diana.

The discussion closed with the accustomed pro and con upon the wart of Cromwell's nose, Realism rejoicing in it, Idealism objecting.

Arthur Rhodes was bidden to stretch his legs on a walk along the heights in the afternoon, and Emma was further vexed by hearing Tony complain of Redworth's treatment of the lad, whom he would not assist to any of the snug little posts he was notoriously able to dispense.

'He has talked of Mr. Rhodes to me,' said Emma. 'He thinks the profession of literature a delusion, and doubts the wisdom of having poets for clerks.'

'John-Bullish!' Diana exclaimed. 'He speaks contemptuously of the poor boy.'

'Only inasmuch as the foolishness of the young man in throwing up the Law provokes his practical mind to speak.'

'He might take my word for the "young man's" ability. I want him to have the means of living, that he may write. He has genius.'

'He may have it. I like him, and have said so. If he were to go back to his law-stool, I have no doubt that Redworth would manage to help him.'

'And make a worthy ancient Braddock of a youth of splendid promise! Have I sketched him too Saxon?'

'It is the lens, and hot the tribe, Tony.'

THE CANTATRICE was not alluded to any more; but Emma's disapproval blocked the current of composition, already subject to chokings in the brain of the author. Diana stayed three days at Copsley, one longer than she had intended, so that Arthur Rhodes might have his fill of country air.

'I would keep him, but I should be no companion for him,' Emma said.

'I suspect the gallant squire is only to be satisfied by landing me safely,' said Diana, and that small remark grated, though Emma saw the simple meaning. When they parted, she kissed her Tony many times. Tears were in her eyes. It seemed to Diana that she was anxious to make amends for the fit of alienation, and she was kissed in return warmly, quite forgiven, notwithstanding the deadly blank she had caused in the imagination of the writer for pay, distracted by the squabbles of Debit and Credit.

Diana chatted spiritedly to young Rhodes on their drive to the train. She was profoundly discouraged by Emma's disapproval of her work. It wanted but that one drop to make a recurrence to the work impossible. There it must lie! And what of the aspects of her household?—Perhaps, after all, the Redworths of the world are right, and Literature as a profession is a delusive pursuit. She did not assent to it without hostility to the world's Redworths.—'They have no sensitiveness, we have too much. We are made of bubbles that a wind will burst, and as the wind is always blowing, your practical Redworths have their crow of us.'

She suggested advice to Arthur Rhodes upon the prudence of his resuming the yoke of the Law.

He laughed at such a notion, saying that he had some expectations of money to come.

'But I fear,' said he, 'that Lady Dunstane is very very ill. She begged me to keep her informed of your address.'

Diana told him he was one of those who should know it whithersoever she went. She spoke impulsively, her sentiments of friendliness for the youth being temporarily brightened by the strangeness of Emma's conduct in deputing it to him to fulfil a duty she had never omitted. 'What can she think I am going to do!'

On her table at home lay, a letter from Mr Warwick. She read it hastily in the presence of Arthur Rhodes, having at a glance at the handwriting anticipated the proposal it contained and the official phrasing.

Her gallant squire was invited to dine with her that evening, costume excused.

They conversed of Literature as a profession, of poets dead and living, of politics, which he abhorred and shied at, and of his prospects.

He wrote many rejected pages, enjoyed an income of eighty pounds per annum, and eked out a subsistence upon the modest sum his pen procured him; a sum extremely insignificant; but great Nature was his own, the world was tributary to him, the future his bejewelled and expectant bride. Diana envied his youthfulness. Nothing is more enviable, nothing richer to the mind, than the aspect of a cheerful poverty. How much nobler it was, contrasted with Redworth's amassing of wealth!

When alone, she went to her bedroom and tried to write, tried to sleep. Mr. Warwick's letter was looked at. It seemed to indicate a threat; but for the moment it did not disturb her so much as the review of her moral prostration. She wrote some lines to her lawyers, quoting one of Mr. Warwick's sentences. That done, his letter was dismissed. Her intolerable languor became alternately a defeating drowsiness and a fever. She succeeded in the effort to smother the absolute cause: it was not suffered to show a front; at the cost of her knowledge of a practised self-deception. 'I wonder whether the world is as bad as a certain class of writers tell us!' she sighed in weariness, and mused on their soundings and probings of poor humanity, which the world accepts for the very bottom truth if their dredge brings up sheer refuse of the abominable. The world imagines those to be at our nature's depths who are impudent enough to expose its muddy shallows. She was in the mood for such a kind of writing: she could have started on it at once but that the theme was wanting; and it may count on popularity, a great repute for penetration. It is true of its kind, though the dredging of nature is the miry form of art. When it flourishes we may be assured we have been overenamelling the higher forms. She felt, and shuddered to feel, that she could draw from dark stores. Hitherto in her works it had been a triumph of the good. They revealed a gaping deficiency of the subtle insight she now possessed. 'Exhibit humanity as it is, wallowing, sensual, wicked, behind the mask,' a voice called to her; she was allured by the contemplation of the wide-mouthed old dragon Ego, whose portrait, decently painted, establishes an instant touch of exchange between author and public, the latter detected and confessing. Next to the pantomime of Humour and Pathos, a cynical surgical knife at the human bosom seems the surest talisman for this agreeable exchange; and she could cut. She gave herself a taste of her powers. She cut at herself mercilessly, and had to bandage the wound in a hurry to keep in life.

Metaphors were her refuge. Metaphorically she could allow her mind to distinguish the struggle she was undergoing, sinking under it. The banished of Eden had to put on metaphors, and the common use of them has helped largely to civilize us. The sluggish in intellect detest them, but our civilization is not much indebted to that major faction. Especially are they needed by the pedestalled woman in her conflict with the natural. Diana saw herself through the haze she conjured up. 'Am I worse than other women?' was a piercing twithought. Worse, would be hideous isolation. The not worse, abased her sex. She could afford to say that the world was bad: not that women were.

Sinking deeper, an anguish of humiliation smote her to a sense of drowning. For what of the poetic ecstasy on her Salvatore heights had not been of origin divine? had sprung from other than spiritual founts? had sprung from the reddened sources she was compelled to conceal? Could it be? She would not believe it. But there was matter to clip her wings, quench her light, in the doubt.

She fell asleep like the wrecked flung ashore.

Danvers entered her room at an early hour for London to inform her that Mr. Percy Dacier was below, and begged permission to wait.

Diana gave orders for breakfast to be proposed to him. She lay staring at the wall until it became too visibly a reflection of her mind.

CHAPTER XXV.
ONCE MORE THE CROSSWAYS AND A CHANGE OF TURNINGS

The suspicion of his having come to impart the news of his proximate marriage ultimately endowed her with sovereign calmness. She had need to think it, and she did. Tea was brought to her while she dressed; she descended the stairs revolving phrases of happy congratulation and the world's ordinary epigrams upon the marriage-tie, neatly mixed.

They read in one another's faces a different meaning from the empty words of excuse and welcome. Dacier's expressed the buckling of a strong set purpose; but, grieved by the look of her eyes, he wasted a moment to say: 'You have not slept. You have heard . . . ?'

'What?' said she, trying to speculate; and that was a sufficient answer.

'I hadn't the courage to call last night; I passed the windows. Give me your hand, I beg.'

She gave her hand in wonderment, and more wonderingly felt it squeezed. Her heart began the hammerthump. She spoke an unintelligible something; saw herself melting away to utter weakness-pride, reserve, simple prudence, all going; crumbled ruins where had stood a fortress imposing to men. Was it love? Her heart thumped shiveringly.

He kept her hand, indifferent to the gentle tension.

'This is the point: I cannot live without you: I have gone on . . . Who was here last night? Forgive me.'

'You know Arthur Rhodes.'

'I saw him leave the door at eleven. Why do you torture me? There's no time to lose now. You will be claimed. Come, and let us two cut the knot. It is the best thing in the world for me—the only thing.

Be brave! I have your hand. Give it for good, and for heaven's sake don't play the sex. Be yourself. Dear soul of a woman! I never saw the soul in one but in you. I have waited: nothing but the dread of losing you sets me speaking now. And for you to be sacrificed a second time to that—! Oh, no! You know you can trust me. On my honour, I take breath from you. You are my better in everything—guide, goddess, dearest heart! Trust me; make me master of your fate.'

'But my friend!' the murmur hung in her throat. He was marvellously transformed; he allowed no space for the arts of defence and evasion.

'I wish I had the trick of courting. There's not time; and I'm a simpleton at the game. We can start this evening. Once away, we leave it to them to settle the matter, and then you are free, and mine to the death.'

'But speak, speak! What is it?' Diana said.

'That if we delay, I'm in danger of losing you altogether.'

Her eyes lightened: 'You mean that you have heard he has determined—?'

'There's a process of the law. But stop it. Just this one step, and it ends. Whether intended or not, it hangs over you, and you will be perpetually tormented. Why waste your whole youth?—and mine as well! For I am bound to you as much as if we had stood at the altar—where we will stand together the instant you are free.'

'But where have you heard . . . ?'

'From an intimate friend. I will tell you—sufficiently intimate—from Lady Wathin. Nothing of a friend, but I see this woman at times. She chose to speak of it to me it doesn't matter why. She is in his confidence, and pitched me a whimpering tale. Let those people chatter. But it's exactly for those people that you are hanging in chains, all your youth shrivelling. Let them shout their worst! It's the bark of a day; and you won't hear it; half a year, and it will be over, and I shall bring you back—the husband of the noblest bride in Christendom! You don't mistrust me?'

'It is not that,' said she. 'But now drop my hand. I am imprisoned.'

'It's asking too much. I've lost you—too many times. I have the hand and I keep it. I take nothing but the hand. It's the hand I want. I give you mine. I love you. Now I know what love is!—and the word carries nothing of its weight. Tell me you do not doubt my honour.'

'Not at all. But be rational. I must think, and I cannot while you keep my hand.'

He kissed it. 'I keep my own against the world.'

A cry of rebuke swelled to her lips at his conqueror's tone. It was not uttered, for directness was in his character and his wooing loyal—save for bitter circumstances, delicious to hear; and so narrow was the ring he had wound about her senses, that her loathing of the circumstances pushed her to acknowledge within her bell of a heart her love for him.

He was luckless enough to say: 'Diana!'

It rang horridly of her husband. She drew her hand to loosen it, with repulsing brows. 'Not that name!'

Dacier was too full of his honest advocacy of the passionate lover to take a rebuff. There lay his unconscious mastery, where the common arts of attack would have tripped him with a quick-witted woman, and where a man of passion, not allowing her to succumb in dignity, would have alarmed her to the breaking loose from him.

'Lady Dunstane calls you Tony.'

'She is my dearest and oldest friend.'

'You and I don't count by years. You are the dearest to me on earth, Tony!'

She debated as to forbidding that name.

The moment's pause wrapped her in a mental hurricane, out of which she came with a heart stopped, her olive cheeks ashen-hued. She had seen that the step was possible.

'Oh! Percy, Percy, are we mad?'

'Not mad. We take what is ours. Tell me, have I ever, ever disrespected you? You were sacred to me; and you are, though now the change has come. Look back on it—it is time lost, years that are dust. But look forward, and you cannot imagine our separation. What I propose is plain sense for us two. Since Rovio, I have been at your feet. Have I not some just claim for recompense? Tell me! Tony!'

The sweetness of the secret name, the privileged name, in his mouth stole through her blood, melting resistance.

She had consented. The swarthy flaming of her face avowed it even more than the surrender of her hand. He gained much by claiming little: he respected her, gave her no touches of fright and shame; and it was her glory to fall with pride. An attempt at a caress would have awakened her view of the whitherward: but she was treated as a sovereign lady rationally advised.

'Is it since Rovio, Percy?'

'Since the morning when you refused me one little flower.'

'If I had given it, you might have been saved!'

'I fancy I was doomed from the beginning.'

'I was worth a thought?'

'Worth a life! worth ten thousand!'

'You have reckoned it all like a sane man:—family, position, the world, the scandal?'

'All. I have long known that you were the mate for me. You have to weather a gale, Tony. It won't last. My dearest! it won't last many months. I regret the trial for you, but I shall be with you, burning for the day to reinstate you and show you the queen you are.'

'Yes, we two can have no covert dealings, Percy,' said Diana. They would be hateful—baseness! Rejecting any baseness, it seemed to her that she stood in some brightness. The light was of a lurid sort. She called on her heart to glory in it as the light of tried love, the love that defied the world. Her heart rose. She and he would at a single step give proof of their love for one another—and this kingdom of love—how different from her recent craven languors!—this kingdom awaited her, was hers for one word; and beset with the oceans of enemies, it was unassailable. If only they were true to the love they vowed, no human force could subvert it: and she doubted him as little as of herself. This new kingdom of love, never entered by her, acclaiming her, was well-nigh unimaginable, in spite of the many hooded messengers it had despatched to her of late. She could hardly believe that it had come.

'But see me as I am,' she said; she faltered it through her direct gaze on him.

'With chains to strike off? Certainly; it is done,' he replied.

'Rather heavier than those of the slave-market! I am the deadest of burdens. It means that your enemies, personal—if you have any, and political—you have numbers; will raise a cry .... Realize it. You may still be my friend. I forgive the bit of wildness.'

She provoked a renewed kissing of her hand; for magnammity in love is an overflowing danger; and when he said: 'The burden you have to bear outweighs mine out of all comparison. What is it to a man—a public man or not! The woman is always the victim. That's why I have held myself in so long:—her strung frame softened. She half yielded to the tug on her arm.

'Is there no talking for us without foolishness?' she murmured. The foolishness had wafted her to sea, far from sight of land. 'Now sit, and speak soberly. Discuss the matter.—Yes, my hand, but I must have my wits. Leave me free to use them till we choose our path. Let it be the brains between us, as far as it can. You ask me to join my fate to yours. It signifies a sharp battle for you, dear friend; perhaps the blighting of the most promising life in England. One question is, can I countervail the burden I shall be, by such help to you as I can afford? Burden, is no word—I rake up a buried fever. I have partially lived it down, and instantly I am covered with spots. The old false charges and this plain offence make a monster of me.'

'And meanwhile you are at the disposal of the man who falsely charged you and armed the world against you,' said Dacier.

'I can fly. The world is wide.'

'Time slips. Your youth is wasted. If you escape the man, he will have triumphed in keeping you from me. And I thirst for you; I look to you for aid and counsel; I want my mate. You have not to be told how you inspire me? I am really less than half myself without you. If I am to do anything in the world, it must be with your aid, you beside me. Our hands are joined: one leap! Do you not see that after .. . well, it cannot be friendship. It imposes rather more on me than I can bear. You are not the woman to trifle; nor I; Tony, the man for it with a woman like you. You are my spring of wisdom. You interdict me altogether—can you?—or we unite our fates, like these hands now. Try to get yours away!'

Her effort ended in a pressure. Resistance, nay, to hesitate at the joining of her life with his after her submission to what was a scorching fire in memory, though it was less than an embrace, accused her of worse than foolishness.

'Well, then,' said she, 'wait three days. Deliberate. Oh! try to know yourself, for your clear reason to guide you. Let us be something better than the crowd abusing us, not simple creatures of impulse—as we choose to call the animal. What if we had to confess that we took to our heels the moment the idea struck us! Three days. We may then pretend to a philosophical resolve. Then come to me: or write to me.'

'How long is it since the old Rovio morning, Tony?'

'An age.'

'Date my deliberations from that day.'

The thought of hers having to be dated possibly from an earlier day, robbed her of her summit of feminine isolation, and she trembled, chilled and flushed; she lost all anchorage.

'So it must be to-morrow,' said he, reading her closely, 'not later. Better at once. But women are not to be hurried.'

'Oh! don't class me, Percy, pray! I think of you, not of myself.'

'You suppose that in a day or two I might vary?'

She fixed her eyes on him, expressing certainty of his unalterable stedfastness. The look allured. It changed: her head shook. She held away and said: 'No, leave me; leave me, dear, dear friend. Percy, my dearest! I will not "play the sex." I am yours if . . . if it is your wish. It may as well be to-morrow. Here I am useless; I cannot write, not screw a thought from my head. I dread that "process of the Law" a second time. To-morrow, if it must be. But no impulses. Fortune is blind; she may be kind to us. The blindness of Fortune is her one merit, and fools accuse her of it, and they profit by it! I fear we all of us have our turn of folly: we throw the stake for good luck. I hope my sin is not very great. I know my position is desperate. I feel a culprit. But I am sure I have courage, perhaps brains to help. At any rate, I may say this: I bring no burden to my lover that he does not know of.'

Dacier pressed her hand. 'Money we shall have enough. My uncle has left me fairly supplied.'

'What would he think?' said Diana, half in a glimpse of meditation.

'Think me the luckiest of the breeched. I fancy I hear him thanking you for "making a man" of me.'

She blushed. Some such phrase might have been spoken by Lord Dannisburgh.

'I have but a poor sum of money,' she said. 'I may be able to write abroad. Here I cannot—if I am to be persecuted.'

'You shall write, with a new pen!' said Dacier. 'You shall live, my darling Tony. You have been held too long in this miserable suspension, neither maid nor wife, neither woman nor stockfish. Ah! shameful. But we 'll right it. The step, for us, is the most reasonable that could be considered. You shake your head. But the circumstances make it so. Courage, and we come to happiness! And that, for you and me, means work. Look at the case of Lord and Lady Dulac. It's identical, except that she is no match beside you: and I do not compare her antecedents with yours. But she braved the leap, and forced the world to swallow it, and now, you see, she's perfectly honoured. I know a place on a peak of the Maritime Alps, exquisite in summer, cool, perfectly solitary, no English, snow round us, pastures at our feet, and the Mediterranean below. There! my Tony. To-morrow night we start. You will meet me-shall I call here?— well, then at the railway station, the South-Eastern, for Paris: say, twenty minutes to eight. I have your pledge? You will come?'

She sighed it, then said it firmly, to be worthy of him. Kind Fortune, peeping under the edge of her bandaged eyes, appeared willing to bestow the beginning of happiness upon one who thought she had a claim to a small taste of it before she died. It seemed distinguishingly done, to give a bite of happiness to the starving!

'I fancied when you were announced that you came for congratulations upon your approaching marriage, Percy.'

'I shall expect to hear them from you to-morrow evening at the station, dear Tony,' said he.

The time was again stated, the pledge repeated. He forbore entreaties for privileges, and won her gratitude.

They named once more the place of meeting and the hour: more significant to them than phrases of intensest love and passion. Pressing hands sharply for pledge of good faith, they sundered.

She still had him in her eyes when he had gone. Her old world lay shattered; her new world was up without a dawn, with but one figure, the sun of it, to light the swinging strangeness.

Was ever man more marvellously transformed? or woman more wildly swept from earth into the clouds? So she mused in the hum of her tempest of heart and brain, forgetful of the years and the conditions preparing both of them for this explosion.

She had much to do: the arrangements to dismiss her servants, write to house-agents and her lawyer, and write fully to Emma, write the enigmatic farewell to the Esquarts and Lady Pennon, Mary Paynham, Arthur Rhodes, Whitmonby (stanch in friendship, but requiring friendly touches), Henry Wilmers, and Redworth. He was reserved to the last, for very enigmatical adieux: he would hear the whole story from Emma; must be left to think as he liked.

The vague letters were excellently well composed: she was going abroad, and knew not when she would return; bade her friends think the best they could of her in the meantime. Whitmonby was favoured with an anecdote, to be read as an apologue by the light of subsequent events. But the letter to Emma tasked Diana. Intending to write fully, her pen committed the briefest sentences: the tenderness she felt for Emma wakening her heart to sing that she was loved, loved, and knew love at last; and Emma's foreseen antagonism to the love and the step it involved rendered her pleadings in exculpation a stammered confession of guiltiness, ignominious, unworthy of the pride she felt in her lover. 'I am like a cartridge rammed into a gun, to be discharged at a certain hour tomorrow,' she wrote; and she sealed a letter so frigid that she could not decide to post it. All day she imagined hearing a distant cannonade. The light of the day following was not like earthly light. Danvers assured her there was no fog in London.

'London is insupportable; I am going to Paris, and shall send for you in a week or two,' said Diana.

'Allow me to say, ma'am, that you had better take me with you,' said Danvers.

'Are you afraid of travelling by yourself, you foolish creature?'

'No, ma'am, but I don't like any hands to undress and dress my mistress but my own.'

'I have not lost the art,' said Diana, chafing for a magic spell to extinguish the woman, to whom, immediately pitying her, she said: 'You are a good faithful soul. I think you have never kissed me. Kiss me on the forehead.'

Danvers put her lips to her mistress's forehead, and was asked: 'You still consider yourself attached to my fortunes?'

'I do, ma'am, at home or abroad; and if you will take me with you ..'

'Not for a week or so.'

'I shall not be in the way, ma'am.'

They played at shutting eyes. The petition of Danvers was declined; which taught her the more; and she was emboldened to say: 'Wherever my mistress goes, she ought to have her attendant with her.' There was no answer to it but the refusal.

The hours crumbled slowly, each with a blow at the passages of retreat. Diana thought of herself as another person, whom she observed, not counselling her, because it was a creature visibly pushed by the Fates. In her own mind she could not perceive a stone of solidity anywhere, nor a face that had the appearance of our common life. She heard the cannon at intervals. The things she said set Danvers laughing, and she wondered at the woman's mingled mirth and stiffness. Five o'clock struck. Her letters were sent to the post. Her boxes were piled from stairs to door. She read the labels, for her goodbye to the hated name of Warwick:—why ever adopted! Emma might well have questioned why! Women are guilty of such unreasoning acts! But this was the close to that chapter. The hour of six went by. Between six and seven came a sound of knocker and bell at the streetdoor. Danvers rushed into the sitting-room to announce that it was Mr. Redworth. Before a word could be mustered, Redworth was in the room. He said: 'You must come with me at once!'

CHAPTER XXVI.
IN WHICH A DISAPPOINTED LOVER RECEIVES A MULTITUDE OF LESSONS

Dacier welted at the station, a good figure of a sentinel over his luggage and a spy for one among the inpouring passengers. Tickets had been confidently taken, the private division of the carriages happily secured. On board the boat she would be veiled. Landed on French soil, they threw off disguises, breasted the facts. And those? They lightened. He smarted with his eagerness.

He had come well in advance of the appointed time, for he would not have had her hang about there one minute alone.

Strange as this adventure was to a man of prominent station before the world, and electrical as the turning-point of a destiny that he was given to weigh deliberately and far-sightedly, Diana's image strung him to the pitch of it. He looked nowhere but ahead, like an archer putting hand for his arrow.

Presently he compared his watch and the terminus clock. She should now be arriving. He went out to meet her and do service. Many cabs and carriages were peered into, couples inspected, ladies and their maids, wives and their husbands—an August exodus to the Continent. Nowhere the starry she. But he had a fund of patience. She was now in some block of the streets. He was sure of her, sure of her courage. Tony and recreancy could not go together. Now that he called her Tony, she was his close comrade, known; the name was a caress and a promise, breathing of her, as the rose of sweetest earth. He counted it to be a month ere his family would have wind of the altered position of his affairs, possibly a year to the day of his making the dear woman his own in the eyes of the world. She was dear past computation, womanly, yet quite unlike the womanish woman, unlike the semi-males courteously called dashing, unlike the sentimental. His present passion for her lineaments, declared her surpassingly beautiful, though his critical taste was rather for the white statue that gave no warmth. She had brains and ardour, she had grace and sweetness, a playful petulancy enlivening our atmosphere, and withal a refinement, a distinction, not to be classed; and justly might she dislike the being classed. Her humour was a perennial refreshment, a running well, that caught all the colours of light; her wit studded the heavens of the recollection of her. In his heart he felt that it was a stepping down for the brilliant woman to give him her hand; a condescension and an act of valour. She who always led or prompted when they conversed, had now in her generosity abandoned the lead and herself to him, and she deserved his utmost honouring.

But where was she? He looked at his watch, looked at the clock. They said the same: ten minutes to the moment of the train's departure.

A man may still afford to dwell on the charms and merits of his heart's mistress while he has ten minutes to spare. The dropping minutes, however, detract one by one from her individuality and threaten to sink her in her sex entirely. It is the inexorable clock that says she is as other women. Dacier began to chafe. He was unaccustomed to the part he was performing:—and if she failed him? She would not. She would be late, though. No, she was in time! His long legs crossed the platform to overtake a tall lady veiled and dressed in black. He lifted his hat; he heard an alarmed little cry and retired. The clock said, Five minutes: a secret chiromancy in addition indicating on its face the word Fool. An odd word to be cast at him! It rocked the icy pillar of pride in the background of his nature. Certainly standing solos at the hour of eight P.M., he would stand for a fool. Hitherto he had never allowed a woman to chance to posture him in that character. He strode out, returned, scanned every lady's shape, and for a distraction watched the veiled lady whom he had accosted. Her figure suggested pleasant features. Either she was disappointed or she was an adept. At the shutting of the gates she glided through, not without a fearful look around and at him. She disappeared. Dacier shrugged. His novel assimilation to the rat-rabble of amatory intriguers tapped him on the shoulder unpleasantly. A luckless member of the fraternity too! The bell, the clock and the train gave him his title. 'And I was ready to fling down everything for the woman!' The trial of a superb London gentleman's resources in the love-passion could not have been much keener. No sign of her.

He who stands ready to defy the world, and is baffled by the absence of his fair assistant, is the fool doubled, so completely the fool that he heads the universal shout; he does not spare himself. The sole consolation he has is to revile the sex. Women! women! Whom have they not made a fool of! His uncle as much as any—and professing to know them. Him also! the man proud of escaping their wiles. 'For this woman . . . !' he went on saying after he had lost sight of her in her sex's trickeries. The nearest he could get to her was to conceive that the arrant coquette was now laughing at her utter subjugation and befooling of the man popularly supposed invincible. If it were known of him! The idea of his being a puppet fixed for derision was madly distempering. He had only to ask the affirmative of Constance Asper to-morrow! A vision of his determination to do it, somewhat comforted him.

Dacier walked up and down the platform, passing his pile of luggage, solitary and eloquent on the barrow. Never in his life having been made to look a fool, he felt the red heat of the thing, as a man who has not blessedly become acquainted with the swish in boyhood finds his untempered blood turn to poison at a blow; he cannot healthily take a licking. But then it had been so splendid an insanity when he urged Diana to fly with him. Any one but a woman would have appreciated the sacrifice.

His luggage had to be removed. He dropped his porter a lordly fee and drove home. From that astonished solitude he strolled to his Club. Curiosity mastering the wrath it was mixed with, he left his Club and crossed the park southward in the direction of Diana's house, abusing her for her inveterate attachment to the regions of Westminster. There she used to receive Lord Dannisburgh; innocently, no doubt-assuredly quite innocently; and her husband had quitted the district. Still it was rather childish for a woman to-be always haunting the seats of Parliament. Her disposition to imagine that she was able to inspire statesmen came in for a share of ridicule; for when we know ourselves to be ridiculous, a retort in kind, unjust upon consideration, is balm. The woman dragged him down to the level of common men; that was the peculiar injury, and it swept her undistinguished into the stream of women. In appearance, as he had proved to the fellows at his Club, he was perfectly self-possessed, mentally distracted and bitter, hating himself for it, snapping at the cause of it. She had not merely disappointed, she had slashed his high conceit of himself, curbed him at the first animal dash forward, and he champed the bit with the fury of a thwarted racer.

Twice he passed her house. Of course no light was shown at her windows. They were scanned malignly.

He held it due to her to call and inquire whether there was any truth in the report of Mrs. Warwick's illness. Mrs. Warwick! She meant to keep the name.

A maid-servant came to the door with a candle in her hand revealing red eyelids. She was not aware that her mistress was unwell. Her mistress had left home some time after six o'clock with a gentleman. She was unable to tell him the gentleman's name. William, the footman, had opened the door to him. Her mistress's maid Mrs. Danvers had gone to the Play—with William. She thought that Mrs. Danvers might know who the gentleman was. The girl's eyelids blinked, and she turned aside. Dacier consoled her with a piece of gold, saying he would come and see Mrs. Danvers in the morning.

His wrath was partially quieted by the new speculations offered up to it. He could not conjure a suspicion of treachery in Diana Warwick; and a treachery so foully cynical! She had gone with a gentleman. He guessed on all sides; he struck at walls, as in complete obscurity.

The mystery of her conduct troubling his wits for the many hours was explained by Danvers. With a sympathy that she was at pains to show, she informed him that her mistress was not at all unwell, and related of how Mr. Redworth had arrived just when her mistress was on the point of starting for Paris and the Continent; because poor Lady Dunstane was this very day to undergo an operation under the surgeons at Copsley, and she did not wish her mistress to be present, but Mr. Redworth thought her mistress ought to be there, and he had gone down thinking she was there, and then came back in hot haste to fetch her, and was just in time, as it happened, by two or three minutes.

Dacier rewarded the sympathetic woman for her intelligence, which appeared to him to have shot so far as to require a bribe. Gratitude to the person soothing his unwontedly ruffled temper was the cause of the indiscretion in the amount he gave.

It appeared to him that he ought to proceed to Copsley for tidings of Lady Dunstane. Thither he sped by the handy railway and a timely train. He reached the parkgates at three in the afternoon, telling his flyman to wait. As he advanced by short cuts over the grass, he studied the look of the rows of windows. She was within, and strangely to his clouded senses she was no longer Tony, no longer the deceptive woman he could in justice abuse. He and she, so close to union, were divided. A hand resembling the palpable interposition of Fate had swept them asunder. Having the poorest right—not any—to reproach her, he was disarmed, he felt himself a miserable intruder; he summoned his passion to excuse him, and gained some unsatisfied repose of mind by contemplating its devoted sincerity; which roused an effort to feel for the sufferer—Diana Warwick's friend. With the pair of surgeons named, the most eminent of their day, in attendance, the case must be serious. To vindicate the breaker of her pledge, his present plight likewise assured him of that, and nearing the house he adopted instinctively the funeral step and mood, just sensible of a novel smallness. For the fortifying testimony of his passion had to be put aside, he was obliged to disavow it for a simpler motive if he applied at the door. He stressed the motive, produced the sentiment, and passed thus naturally into hypocrisy, as lovers precipitated by their blood among the crises of human conditions are often forced to do. He had come to inquire after Lady Dunstane. He remembered that it had struck him as a duty, on hearing of her dangerous illness.

The door opened before he touched the bell. Sir Lukin knocked against him and stared.

'Ah!—who—?—you?' he said, and took him by the arm and pressed him on along the gravel. 'Dacier, are you? Redworth's in there. Come on a step, come! It's the time for us to pray. Good God! There's mercy for sinners. If ever there was a man! . . . But, oh, good God! she's in their hands this minute. My saint is under the knife.'

Dacier was hurried forward by a powerful hand. 'They say it lasts about five minutes, four and a half—or more! My God! When they turned me out of her room, she smiled to keep me calm. She said: "Dear husband": the veriest wretch and brutallest husband ever poor woman . . . and a saint! a saint on earth! Emmy!' Tears burst from him.

He pulled forth his watch and asked Dacier for the time.

'A minute's gone in a minute. It's three minutes and a half. Come faster. They're at their work! It's life or death. I've had death about me. But for a woman! and your wife! and that brave soul! She bears it so. Women are the bravest creatures afloat. If they make her shriek, it'll be only if she thinks I 'm out of hearing. No: I see her. She bears it!—They mayn't have begun yet. It may all be over! Come into the wood. I must pray. I must go on my knees.'

Two or three steps in the wood, at the mossed roots of a beech, he fell kneeling, muttering, exclaiming.

The tempest of penitence closed with a blind look at his watch, which he left dangling. He had to talk to drug his thoughts.

'And mind you,' said he, when he had rejoined Dacier and was pushing his arm again, rounding beneath the trees to a view of the house, 'for a man steeped in damnable iniquity! She bears it all for me, because I begged her, for the chance of her living. It's my doing—this knife! Macpherson swears there is a chance. Thomson backs him. But they're at her, cutting! . . . The pain must be awful—the mere pain! The gentlest creature ever drew breath! And women fear blood—and her own! And a head! She ought to have married the best man alive, not a—! I can't remember her once complaining of me—not once. A common donkey compared to her! All I can do is to pray. And she knows the beast I am, and has forgiven me. There isn't a blessed text of Scripture that doesn't cry out in praise of her. And they cut and hack . . . !' He dropped his head. The vehement big man heaved, shuddering. His lips worked fast.

'She is not alone with them, unsupported?' said Dacier.

Sir Lukin moaned for relief. He caught his watch swinging and stared at it. 'What a good fellow you were to come! Now 's the time to know your friends. There's Diana Warwick, true as steel. Redworth came on her tiptoe for the Continent; he had only to mention . . . Emmy wanted to spare her. She would not have sent—wanted to spare her the sight. I offered to stand by . . . Chased me out. Diana Warwick's there:— worth fifty of me! Dacier, I've had my sword-blade tried by Indian horsemen, and I know what true as steel means. She's there. And I know she shrinks from the sight of blood. My oath on it, she won't quiver a muscle! Next to my wife, you may take my word for it, Dacier, Diana Warwick is the pick of living women. I could prove it.

They go together. I could prove it over and over. She's the loyallest woman anywhere. Her one error was that marriage of hers, and how she ever pitched herself into it, none of us can guess.' After a while, he said: 'Look at your watch.'

'Nearly twenty minutes gone.'

'Are they afraid to send out word? It's that window !' He covered his eyes, and muttered, sighed. He became abruptly composed in appearance. 'The worst of a black sheep like me is, I'm such an infernal sinner, that Providence! . . . But both surgeons gave me their word of honour that there was a chance. A chance! But it's the end of me if Emmy . . . . Good God! no! the knife's enough; don't let her be killed! It would be murder. Here am I talking! I ought to be praying. I should have sent for the parson to help me; I can't get the proper words—bellow like a rascal trooper strung up for the cat. It must be twenty-five minutes now. Who's alive now!'

Dacier thought of the Persian Queen crying for news of the slaughtered, with her mind on her lord and husband: 'Who is not dead?' Diana exalted poets, and here was an example of the truth of one to nature, and of the poor husband's depth of feeling. They said not the same thing, but it was the same cry de profundis.

He saw Redworth coming at a quick pace.

Redworth raised his hand. Sir Lukin stopped. 'He's waving!'

'It's good,' said Dacier.

'Speak! are you sure?'

'I judge by the look.'

Redworth stepped unfalteringly.

'It's over, all well,' he said. He brushed his forehead and looked sharply cheerful.

'My dear fellow! my dear fellow!' Sir Lukin grasped his hand. 'It's more than I deserve. Over? She has borne it! She would have gone to heaven and left me!

Is she safe?'

'Doing well.'

'Have you seen the surgeons?'

'Mrs. Warwick.'

'What did she say?'

'A nod of the head.'

'You saw her?'

'She came to the stairs.'

'Diana Warwick never lies. She wouldn't lie, not with a nod! They've saved Emmy—do you think?'

'It looks well.'

My girl has passed the worst of it?'

'That's over.'

Sir Lukin gazed glassily. The necessity of his agony was to lean to the belief, at a beckoning, that Providence pardoned him, in tenderness for what would have been his loss. He realized it, and experienced a sudden calm: testifying to the positive pardon.

'Now, look here, you two fellows, listen half a moment,' he addressed Redworth and Dacier; 'I've been the biggest scoundrel of a husband unhung, and married to a saint; and if she's only saved to me; I'll swear to serve her faithfully, or may a thunderbolt knock me to perdition! and thank God for his justice! Prayers are answered, mind you, though a fellow may be as black as a sweep. Take a warning from me. I've had my lesson.'

Dacier soon after talked of going. The hope of seeing Diana had abandoned him, the desire was almost extinct.

Sir Lukin could not let him go. He yearned to preach to him or any one from his personal text of the sinner honourably remorseful on account of and notwithstanding the forgiveness of Providence, and he implored Dacier and Redworth by turns to be careful when they married of how they behaved to—the sainted women their wives; never to lend ear to the devil, nor to believe, as he had done, that there is no such thing as a devil, for he had been the victim of him, and he knew. The devil, he loudly proclaimed, has a multiplicity of lures, and none more deadly than when he baits with a petticoat. He had been hooked, and had found the devil in person. He begged them urgently to keep his example in memory. By following this and that wildfire he had stuck himself in a bog—a common result with those who would not see the devil at work upon them; and it required his dear suffering saint to be at death's doors, cut to pieces and gasping, to open his eyes. But, thank heaven, they were opened at last! Now he saw the beast he was: a filthy beast! unworthy of tying his wife's shoestring. No confessions could expose to them the beast he was. But let them not fancy there was no such thing as an active DEVIL about the world.

Redworth divined that the simply sensational man abased himself before Providence and heaped his gratitude on the awful Power in order to render it difficult for the promise of the safety of his wife to be withdrawn.

He said: 'There is good hope'; and drew an admonition upon himself.

'Ah! my dear good Redworth,' Sir Lukin sighed from his elevation of outspoken penitence: 'you will see as I do some day. It is the devil, think as you like of it. When you have pulled down all the Institutions of the Country, what do you expect but ruins? That Radicalism of yours has its day. You have to go through a wrestle like mine to understand it. You say, the day is fine, let's have our game. Old England pays for it! Then you'll find how you love the old land of your birth—the noblest ever called a nation!—with your Corn Law Repeals!—eh, Dacier? —You 'll own it was the devil tempted you. I hear you apologizing. Pray God, it mayn't be too late!'

He looked up at the windows. 'She may be sinking!'

'Have no fears,' Redworth said; 'Mrs. Warwick would send for you.'

'She would. Diana Warwick would be sure to send. Next to my wife, Diana Warwick's . . . she'd send, never fear. I dread that room. I'd rather go through a regiment of sabres—though it 's over now. And Diana Warwick stood it. The worst is over, you told me. By heaven! women are wonderful creatures. But she hasn't a peer for courage. I could trust her—most extraordinary thing; that marriage of hers!—not a soul has ever been able to explain it:—trust her to the death.'

Redworth left them, and Sir Lukin ejaculated on the merits of Diana Warwick to Dacier. He laughed scornfully: 'And that's the woman the world attacks for want of virtue! Why, a fellow hasn't a chance with her, not a chance. She comes out in blazing armour if you unmask a battery. I don't know how it might be if she were in love with a fellow. I doubt her thinking men worth the trouble. I never met the man. But if she were to take fire, Troy 'd be nothing to it. I wonder whether we might go in: I dread the house.'

Dacier spoke of departing.

'No, no, wait,' Sir Lukin begged him. 'I was talking about women. They are the devil—or he makes most use of them: and you must learn to see the cloven foot under their petticoats, if you're to escape them. There's no protection in being in love with your wife; I married for love; I am, I always have been, in love with her; and I went to the deuce. The music struck up and away I waltzed. A woman like Diana Warwick might keep a fellow straight, because she,'s all round you; she's man and woman in brains; and legged like a deer, and breasted like a swan, and a regular sheaf of arrows—in her eyes. Dark women—ah! But she has a contempt for us, you know. That's the secret of her.— Redworth 's at the door. Bad? Is it bad? I never was particularly fond of that house—hated it. I love it now for Emmy's sake. I couldn't live in another—though I should be haunted. Rather her ghost than nothing— though I'm an infernal coward about the next world. But if you're right with religion you needn't fear. What I can't comprehend in Redworth is his Radicalism, and getting richer and richer.'

'It's not a vow of poverty,' said Dacier.

'He'll find they don't coalesce, or his children will. Once the masses are uppermost! It's a bad day, Dacier, when we 've no more gentlemen in the land. Emmy backs him, so I hold my tongue. To-morrow's a Sunday. I wish you were staying here; I 'd take you to church with me-we shirk it when we haven't a care. It couldn't do you harm. I've heard capital sermons. I've always had the good habit of going to church, Dacier. Now 's the time for remembering them. Ah, my dear fellow, I 'm not a parson. It would have been better for me if I had been.'

And for you too! his look added plainly. He longed to preach; he was impelled to chatter.

Redworth reported the patient perfectly quiet, breathing calmly.

'Laudanum?' asked Sir Lukin. 'Now there's a poison we've got to bless! And we set up in our wisdom for knowing what is good for us!'

He had talked his hearers into a stupefied assent to anything he uttered.

'Mrs. Warwick would like to see you in two or three minutes; she will come down,' Redworth said to Dacier.

'That looks well, eh? That looks bravely,' Sir Lukin cried. 'Diana, Warwick wouldn't leave the room without a certainty. I dread the look of those men; I shall have to shake their hands! And so I do, with all my heart: only—But God bless them! But we must go in, if she's coming down.'

They entered the house, and sat in the drawing-room, where Sir Lukin took up from the table one of his wife's Latin books, a Persius, bearing her marginal notes. He dropped his head on it, with sobs.

The voice of Diana recalled him to the present. She counselled him to control himself; in that case he might for one moment go to the chamber- door and assure himself by the silence that his wife was resting. She brought permission from the surgeons and doctor, on his promise to be still.

Redworth supported Sir Lukin tottering out.

Dacier had risen. He was petrified by Diana's face, and thought of her as whirled from him in a storm, bearing the marks of it. Her underlip hung for short breaths; the big drops of her recent anguish still gathered on her brows; her eyes were tearless, lustreless; she looked ancient in youth, and distant by a century, like a tall woman of the vaults, issuing white-ringed, not of our light.

She shut her mouth for strength to speak to him.

He said: 'You are not ill? You are strong?'

'I? Oh, strong. I will sit. I cannot be absent longer than two minutes. The trial of her strength is to come. If it were courage, we might be sure. The day is fine?'

'A perfect August day.'

'I held her through it. I am thankful to heaven it was no other hand than mine. She wished to spare me. She was glad of her Tony when the time came. I thought I was a coward—I could have changed with her to save her; I am a strong woman, fit to submit to that work. I should not have borne it as she did. She expected to sink under it. All her dispositions were made for death-bequests to servants and to . . . to friends: every secret liking they had, thought of!'

Diana clenched her hands.

'I hope!' Dacier said.

'You shall hear regularly. Call at Sir William's house to-morrow. He sleeps here to-night. The suspense must last for days. It is a question of vital power to bear the shock. She has a mind so like a flying spirit that, just before the moment, she made Mr. Lanyan Thomson smile by quoting some saying of her Tony's.'

'Try by-and-by to recollect it,' said Dacier.

'And you were with that poor man! How did he pass the terrible time? I pitied him.'

'He suffered; he prayed.'

'It was the best he could do. Mr. Redworth was as he always is at the trial, a pillar. Happy the friend who knows him for one! He never thinks of himself in a crisis. He is sheer strength to comfort and aid. They will drive you to the station with Mr. Thomson. He returns to relieve Sir William to-morrow. I have learnt to admire the men of the knife! No profession equals theirs in self-command and beneficence. Dr. Bridgenorth is permanent here.'

'I have a fly, and go back immediately,' said Dacier.

'She shall hear of your coming. Adieu.'

Diana gave him her hand. It was gently pressed.

A wonderment at the utter change of circumstances took Dacier passingly at the sight of her vanishing figure.

He left the house, feeling he dared have no personal wishes. It had ceased to be the lover's hypocrisy with him.

The crisis of mortal peril in that house enveloped its inmates, and so wrought in him as to enshroud the stripped outcrying husband, of whom he had no clear recollection, save of the man's agony. The two women, striving against death, devoted in friendship, were the sole living images he brought away; they were a new vision of the world and our life.

He hoped with Diana, bled with her. She rose above him high, beyond his transient human claims. He envied Redworth the common friendly right to be near her. In reflection, long after, her simplicity of speech, washed pure of the blood-emotions, for token of her great nature, during those two minutes of their sitting together, was, dearer, sweeter to the lover than if she had shown by touch or word that a faint allusion to their severance was in her mind; and this despite a certain vacancy it created.

He received formal information of Lady Dunstane's progress to convalescence. By degrees the simply official tone of Diana's letters combined with the ceasing of them and the absence of her personal charm to make a gentleman not remarkable for violence in the passion so calmly reasonable as to think the dangerous presence best avoided for a time. Subject to fits of the passion, he certainly was, but his position in the world was a counselling spouse, jealous of his good name. He did not regret his proposal to take the leap; he would not have regretted it if taken. On the safe side of the abyss, however, it wore a gruesome look to his cool blood.